When Charles Landon dies, the legacy he leaves behind has very different implications for each of his four children. For arrogant CADE LANDON it means a never-to-be-forgotten meeting with ANGELICA GORDON that will change his life forever. What *all* of the Landons find through Landon's Legacy, though, is the key that finally unlocks their hearts to love....

Dear Reader,

Welcome to the exciting world of the Landons, and to the legacy that changes the lives of the entire family.

The idea for these books came to me when a friend and I met for lunch at a restaurant in New York. While we were waiting to be served, I overheard some women talking at the next table. They were discussing what makes a man exciting. "He has to be gorgeous," said one. "And a rebel," said another. "And not the least bit interested in being tamed," said a third. The next thing I knew, Cade, Grant and Zach Landon sprang to life inside my head. They were certainly handsome, rebellious and untameable, and when I wondered what kind of women could possibly put up with them, their beautiful sister Kyra materialized and said, well, she'd always loved them, even if they were impossible.

This month I'm delighted to introduce you to Cade Landon. Cade's never met an oil well or a woman he can't tame...until he heads for Texas and Angelica Gordon shows him a woman can be every bit as stubborn as she is beautiful.

So settle back and enjoy four months of love, laughter and tears as you discover the full meaning of the Landon legacy.

With my very warmest regards,

Sandra Marton

SANDRA MARTON

An Indecent Proposal

Harlequin Books

TORONTO • NEW YORK • LONDON
AMSTERDAM • PARIS • SYDNEY • HAMBURG
STOCKHOLM • ATHENS • TOKYO • MILAN
MADRID • WARSAW • BUDAPEST • AUCKLAND

ISBN 0-373-11808-2

AN INDECENT PROPOSAL

First North American Publication 1996.

Copyright © 1995 by Sandra Myles.

This edition published by arrangement with Harlequin Books S.A.

Printed in U.S.A.

PROLOGUE

IT WAS Cade Landon's twenty-eighth birthday, and his gift from the Sultan of Dumai had been delivered a few minutes ago.

Her name was Leilia, and to say she was beautiful was to say that stars were simply lights in the desert sky.

There'd been a discreet knock at the door to Cade's suite. He'd opened it and something straight out of the Arabian Nights had entered: two robed Bedouins clutching flutes and drums, a serving boy staggering under the weight of a tray laden with what seemed to be every Arabian delicacy imaginable, including a not-so-Arabian bottle of vintage Krug champagne, and a mysterious figure swathed from head to toe in silk.

Cade was puzzled, but only for a second. He'd been granted the honor of a suite on the same floor as the Sultan's private rooms. An error had been made, obviously. This was the Sultan's entertainment for the evening, arrived at his door by mistake.

The Bedouins offered the traditional greeting, touching their hands to their lips and hearts as they bowed low before him.

"*Masa el-kheyr,* my lord," said the man holding the flute.

"Good evening," Cade said, politely returning the greeting. "But I'm afraid there's been a mix-up."

"My lord?"

Cade glanced at the silk-draped figure. The veiling had slipped an inch or two, enough so he could see that he was being watched by a pair of enormous, kohl-rimmed eyes. It looked as if the Sultan was going to have a very pleasant evening indeed, Cade thought, and smiled.

5

"You've come to the wrong place, my friend." He nodded toward the far end of the elegant corridor, its magnificent mosaic floor and carpeted walls lit by enough crystal chandeliers to put the Hall of Mirrors at Versailles to shame. "The Sultan's apartment is—"

"Are you not my Lord Landon?"

"I'm Landon, yes, but—"

"Then we have come to the right place." The little entourage brushed past him and made its way into the sitting room. The boy deposited the tray and scurried out the door. The musicians and the silk-draped figure remained.

Puzzled, Cade thrust his fingers into his sun-streaked chestnut hair. "Look," he said, "I don't mean to be rude, but—"

The sounds of the flute and drum drowned out the rest of his words. Openmouthed, he listened to what sounded like the cries of a cat with its tail caught in a wringer before he realized he was hearing a Mid-Eastern version of "Happy Birthday."

"Dear God," he muttered—and all at once, the music became soft and sensuous.

That was when the lady with the kohl-rimmed eyes had slithered into action, stepping forward and slowly shedding rainbow-colored layers of silk until she'd stood before him wearing a sleeveless silver vest that ended just beneath her breasts, a long, gauzy skirt that began dangerous inches below her jeweled navel, and a smile that promised she intended to be the best damned birthday present a man ever had.

"I am Leilia," she'd purred, "and I am yours to command, my lord."

Now she was circling Cade gracefully, her hips swaying to the music. Tiny bells on her fingers and ankles tinkled as she danced; her hair streamed over her golden skin like an ebony waterfall.

The drumbeat quickened and the girl's movements grew more provocative. Cade watched for a moment and then he turned, popped open the Krug and poured some into a crystal flute. Jesus, he thought, downing the chilled wine in one long mouthful, what was he going to do with her when she finished dancing?

Laughter rose in his throat and he bit it back.

He sure as hell knew what he was supposed to do with her.

She was gorgeous and sexy and, he was sure, well-trained in the art of love.

But Cade had never taken a woman whose favors had been bought. It had never been necessary. Women came easily to him, and always had.

Maybe it was the element of danger that seemed to emanate from him. The broad shoulders and lean, hard body, honed by years spent working on oil rigs, the dark blue eyes that could turn almost black with passion or anger, even the nose that had been broken in a brawl on an offshore rig and left to heal on its own—all of the things that made other men look at Cade with respect made women look at him with longing.

Cade knew it, but there was nothing immodest in his self-assessment. It was simple logic, and he was nothing if not logical when it came to women. He had no time for the foolishness of emotional attachments. His life was far too full for such nonsense.

It suited him that the women he spent time with were invariably beautiful, eager to share his bed and as uninterested in tying themselves down as he was.

Did a woman sent to a man as a gift fall into that category?

Leilia brushed lightly against him as she whirled past. Cade looked at her. Her arms were outstretched, straining the tiny silver vest to its limits. Their eyes met, and she gave him a dazzling smile.

Hell, he thought, and grinned back. No matter how the evening ended, this was going to be a birthday to remember.

And suddenly, incongruously, his thoughts flew back in time to another birthday celebration, seven long years before.

He had been twenty-one, and his father had insisted on throwing a party at their Colorado ranch.

"It'll be the biggest shindig anybody's ever seen, boy," he'd said.

It was that, all right, the sort Denver had come to expect of Charles Landon, just four or five hundred of his closest friends, a full orchestra, a performing magician, a trained chimpanzee that smoked cigars and enough lobster, oysters and caviar to feed a small country.

At midnight, Charles had directed all the guests to the front windows. A hush had fallen over the crowd as a spotlight, mounted for the occasion on one of the mansion's turrets, blazed to life, illuminating a cherry-red Corvette in the curving driveway. It was tied with an enormous silver bow.

"Yours," Charles said brusquely. "Do you like it?"

"Like it? I—I..." Cade shook his head, speechless. He'd dreamed of a car like this since getting his driver's license at sixteen. That his father had bought the 'Vette stunned him. Not the sheer extravagance of the gift— Charles was big on extravagant gestures. It was just that the things he gave his youngest son were never quite the things Cade would have chosen for himself.

The party, for instance. Cade hadn't wanted it. He'd wanted a quiet evening with the girl he'd fallen in love with that summer, an evening he hoped would end with Stacey smiling and saying yes, oh yes, she would marry him and build a life with him, one that would not be dependent on Landon power and money.

Instead, he'd ended up with a bunch of strangers, all intent on cozying up to the richest, most powerful entrepreneur west of the Mississippi—and, to make matters worse, Stacey was nowhere in sight. She'd promised to come to the party, even though Cade knew it would displease his father, who had not hesitated to say what he thought of his youngest son becoming involved with a girl who worked at Landon Enterprises.

"A common employee," was Charles's phrase, meaning she had no background, no money and no connections. "She's not for you, boy," he said a dozen times over, which only made Cade all the more convinced that she was.

"Well?" Charles demanded. "Is the Corvette what you wanted?"

Cade swung toward the older man, a sudden tightness in his throat. The car was surely a symbol of something. His father was recognizing him as a man. Maybe, just maybe, they were finally going to begin to understand each other.

"Yes," he said, "yes, it is. Thank you, Father. Thank you very much. I never expected—"

"Make the most of it, boy."

Cade smiled. "I will."

"You've only got this next semester to play with it." His father chuckled as if he were about to tell a joke. "You won't want to take it to New York with you, after graduation. There's no point in having a car like the 'Vette in that city."

"New York? But I'm not going to New York. Why would you think—"

"We're opening a new office there. You'll work with Switzer, learn how to run it, soon as you graduate."

Cade's eyes narrowed. "I didn't study petroleum geology so I could sit behind a desk. You know that. You agreed—"

"I changed my mind."

"It's too late to change your mind," Cade said sharply. "I've already made plans. I'm going to ask Stacey—"

"Stacey?" his father said, and laughed. "Stacey is on her way to San Francisco."

The tightness in Cade's throat changed, became an iron band that threatened to clamp off his breath.

"What are you talking about?"

"I promoted your girlfriend. I gave her a spot in our West Coast management program, effective immediately."

"No!" Cade's fists clenched, and he took a step toward his father. "Stacey loves me. She wouldn't—"

"Stop being a fool, boy! The girl knows opportunity when she sees it." Charles thrust the Corvette's keys at Cade. "It's time for you to show the same good sense."

It was all a blur after that. Cade could only remember someone—Zach, maybe, or Grant—grabbing his arms and holding him back before he could make a bigger fool of himself than he already had.

Just before dawn, he'd scrawled hasty notes to Kyra, Grant and Zach. Then he'd slipped from the house, leaving behind the red Corvette and his father's determination to rule his life. A bored trucker had picked him up on the highway and taken him as far as Albuquerque. From there, he'd thumbed a ride east to Oklahoma and his first job on an oil rig—if you could call washing greasy dishes for the crew a job on an oil rig, he thought with a tight smile and poured himself some more champagne.

It had been a long, hard road from that night to this one, but he'd traveled it his way. Oh, he'd gone back home to visit eventually, but not until he'd made his first big strike in the Texas oil fields. Charles had greeted him with casual indifference, almost as if he'd never been away. As for what had happened the night of Cade's twenty-first birthday—neither man had ever mentioned it.

Cade's mouth twisted. In a way, he supposed, his father had done him a favor. He'd saved him from ever again confusing love with lust, from tying himself down to one woman when the world was filled with so many, all of them eager to share his bed for as long as their mutual passion lasted.

The music was building to a wild crescendo. Cade's gaze swept over the veiled woman dancing before him. The curve of her breasts was lush, the rounded convexity of her belly alluring. His body tightened. This was what life was all about, he thought, a beautiful woman waiting for you and a job well done.

Yesterday, rich black gold had come shooting out of the earth that had hoarded it for millennia. The Sultan, in his gratitude, had instantly doubled Cade's already outrageous, agreed-upon fee.

Tonight, if he wished, this woman would be his.

The music came to an abrupt halt. Leilia dropped gracefully to the floor at Cade's feet, her forehead pressed to the intricate tilework. He waited a moment, then bent and touched his hand lightly to her hair.

She leaned back and rose to her knees, smiling, her dark eyes filled with promise. The tip of her pink tongue slid slowly across her lips.

"My lord," she whispered, "I am yours."

The door clicked softly shut after the departed musicians. Cade offered the woman his hand. She took it and came slowly to her feet.

"You're very lovely," he said. "And very desirable." He smiled, regretfully knowing what his decision must be. "But—"

"But my lord does not want a woman who has been paid to warm his bed," she said with a little smile.

"It isn't that," he said, although, of course, it was. "I'm tired tonight, that's all, and—"

She moved closer and splayed her hand across the front of his shirt. The bells on her fingers tinkled softly.

"No one has paid for me, my lord. I have watched you these past weeks, working shirtless with your men in the hot sun, and I grew more and more determined to find a way to meet you." A scent rose from her as she moved closer, a heady mix of wild jasmine and woman. "The Sultan arranged for the dancer, Fima, to come to you tonight," Leilia whispered, linking her hands around Cade's neck. "I gave her my favorite necklace so that she would permit me to don her veils and come to you in her place."

Cade felt his body quicken. "Did you?" he murmured.

Leilia laughed softly as she drew his head slowly to hers. "Yes, my lord. I did."

The knock at the door was like a peal of thunder. Cade cursed under his breath as he stepped away from the woman.

"Yes?" he growled. "What is it?"

The door swung open and the Sultan of Dumai stepped into the room. Leilia gasped, dropped a quick curtsy and rushed past the Sultan's bulky body into the hallway, but the man paid no attention to her.

"Your Highness," Cade said. He touched his hand to his lips and heart, determinedly ignoring the tension still coiled within his muscles. "I am honored by your presence, sir. My thanks for your gracious gifts."

"Cade, my friend." The Sultan's moon face was wreathed in sorrow. "I fear that I am the bearer of unhappy news."

Cade's eyes narrowed, all thoughts of the woman quickly forgotten.

"The well," he said sharply. "Is it—"

"The well is fine. The oil flows from it, as you said it would."

Cade blew out his breath. "Hell," he said with a little laugh, "for a minute there I thought—"

"There has been a wire for you, from America." The Sultan put his hand on Cade's arm. "I am afraid your father has passed away."

Cade blinked. "My father? Dead?"

"I am sorry to bring you such news, my friend."

Charles Landon, dead? The old man had been ill for a couple of months but it hadn't been anything serious, Grant had said....

"Is there something I can do to make things easier?"

Cade looked up, cleared his throat. "I, ah, I can't think of— Well, actually... Yeah. I, uh, I'd be grateful if you could arrange for me to get a flight out, as quickly as possible."

"That is not a problem. My private jet will take you home. May I be of assistance in any other way? Do you have calls to make? Arrangements to take care of?"

"No, no, thank you, sir. My brothers will have seen to everything, I'm sure. I just—I can't believe that— that—"

The Sultan nodded. "It is fate," he said softly. "*In Sha'allah.* We are only men, after all, and subject to the whims of God."

He turned and left the room, shutting the door quietly after him. Cade stood still after he'd gone, and then he stuffed his hands into the pockets of his trousers, walked slowly to the windows and stared blindly out into the blackness of the desert night.

In Sha'allah, he thought, with a bitter smile. *In Sha'allah.*

Thousands of miles away, Angelica Gordon stared out her window at the blackness of the Texas night.

Were these the same stars that hung in the sky back home in New England? Angelica smiled. She knew that they were. The stars just looked brighter here.

Her father would have said it was because everything in Texas was bigger and better than it was anywhere else.

Even debts, she thought, her smile fading. The ones at Gordon Oil were mounting so fast they made her head spin. She'd taken over the company flushed with determination, certain she could pull it back from the brink of disaster—but she only seemed to have pushed it closer.

Sooner or later, somebody at Landon Enterprises would notice what was happening to one of its newest acquisitions, and then...

Angelica stepped away from the window. She sighed, sank into an old-fashioned rocker and leaned back. Her hair, loose for the night, fell over her shoulders in a fiery tumble of soft, coppery curls.

If only the men who worked for her, who worked *with* her in this super macho business, would give her a chance. If only they'd stop treating her as if she were an intruder in their private club—but that was about as likely as the moon suddenly dropping from the sky.

This was a world where men flexed their muscles instead of their brains, where they spoke an unintelligible jargon in an incomprehensible drawl and where dressing for dinner meant wearing white Stetson hats and black boots. It was a world where men thought women belonged in the kitchen and in the bedroom. But in the boardroom? Never.

Even her father had thought that way. Oh, Hank Gordon had let her work in his office each summer while she was in college, but whenever she'd suggested he take her on as a full-time employee after graduation, he'd chuckled and patted her on the head as if she'd made some marvelous joke. Eventually she'd had to accept the truth, that he'd never give her a real job at Gordon Oil no matter how many business courses she took or what amount of competency she showed, and she'd gone on to an academic career.

Yet now, thanks to a twist of fate, here she was, running Gordon Oil.

Running it straight into the ground.

Angelica rose from the chair, drew the emerald green robe that was the same color as her eyes more tightly around her slender body and looked out the window again. The stars still blazed in the night sky, as bright and unreachable as they'd ever been.

No, she told herself, no, she was not destroying Gordon Oil! The company's problems had started long before she'd taken over. And she could turn things around. She had everything going for her—determination, and knowledge, and all the plans she'd drawn up over the years—plans her father had never wanted to look at.

All she needed now was for fate—that same fate that had put her into this situation in the first place—to be kind.

Angelica gave a deep sigh.

But who could ever know what fate would bring?

CHAPTER ONE

EARLY morning sunlight streamed through the arched windows of the Landon mansion, lighting the dark corners and spilling golden brilliance on the kilim carpets that covered the oiled parquet floors.

Cade smothered a yawn as he entered the dining room. It was empty, and he smiled to himself as he made straight for the silver coffee service set out on the sideboard.

Some things never changed. There was always fresh coffee on the sideboard—and Landon House was still the biggest, most impressive dwelling on the grassy slopes overlooking Emerald Lake.

"'Mornin', Mr. Cade."

He turned as Stella, who'd been in charge of the kitchen for more years than he could remember, came edging through the service door, pushing a well-laden trolley. Cade moved to help her, but she waved him off.

"You just relax and enjoy your coffee, Mr. Cade." With deft, swift movements, she laid out platters of fruit, cheese, croissants, eggs, waffles, bacon and ham on the sideboard. "How's that?" she said, surveying the mountains of food with obvious satisfaction.

Cade grinned. "What?" he said. "No steak?"

"Did you want steak?"

"God, no," Cade said quickly. "This is fine, Stella. Terrific, in fact."

Stella looked doubtful. "You sure?"

"Who'd want anything more than to start the day with your wonderful coffee?" Cade said, lifting his cup in salute.

Stella blushed prettily. "Your teasin' ways are gonna get you in trouble one of these days, Mr. Cade," she said as she sailed through the door to the kitchen.

Cade hooked a chair out from the table with one booted foot and sank into it, his coffee cup balanced in his strong, tanned hands. Stella always produced a gargantuan breakfast as decreed years before by Charles Landon, even though no one ever put more than a dent into the mountains of food.

Cade sighed. Landon House was still less a home than one man's statement of control—control Charles Landon's sons had all fought against, one way or another.

But others had bowed to his power, right to the end.

Three days ago, at the funeral, the house had been filled with those come to pay final homage. Bankers, judges, captains of finance and industry as well as half a dozen congressmen and senators—they'd all shown up.

"Damn," Zach had mumbled as he'd sidled past Cade late in the afternoon, "it's like a three-ring circus."

Their father would have loved every minute of it, right down to the mile-long stream of Cadillacs, Lincolns and Mercedeses that had followed the hearse to the marble mausoleum where Ellen Landon, who'd died giving birth to Kyra, lay entombed.

But he would never have understood what had happened yesterday, after the formal reading of his will.

The mansion and all its vast acreage had been left to Kyra, along with the bulk of Charles's personal fortune.

Landon Enterprises—the far-flung, multimillion-dollar empire on which Charles had lavished all his attention and energy—had gone to his three sons.

But none of them wanted it.

Cade had been the first to say it, as soon as he and his brothers were alone.

"You can have my share," he'd said bluntly. "I don't want anything to do with the old man's business."

Grant had risen to pour them all a drink. "Always have to be first, don't you, little brother? You took the words right out of my mouth. I don't want my piece, either."

Zach had accepted the cut-glass tumbler of bourbon whiskey Grant held out to him.

"Well," he'd said, "that means the vote's unanimous."

Within minutes, they'd agreed that Zach, whose specialty was finance, would figure out Landon Enterprises's net worth. Grant, whose field was the law, would draw up the necessary legal papers for its sale.

Cade's mouth had twitched when his brothers looked at him.

"I'll find us an oil well to invest the profits in," he'd said, and all three of them had laughed, which had helped ease away the last remaining tension that came of finally acknowledging the painful truth.

They had all, at different times, respected, feared, even hated their father. But none of them had loved him.

After the laughter had faded, Cade had assured his brothers he'd been in a dozen different hellholes where they could use the profits of the sale to build much-needed schools and medical centers.

And so it was over, Cade thought now as he rose and walked to the sideboard, all but the details. Victor Bayliss, their father's administrative assistant, had asked for a breakfast meeting to tie up loose ends.

Thanks to Cade, Grant had got stuck with the job.

"You're the logical one to meet with Bayliss," he'd said with an innocent smile. "Everybody knows it takes a lawyer to talk to a lawyer."

"Thrown to the wolves by my own flesh and blood," Grant had said, but he'd softened the words with a grin.

Cade glanced at the grandfather clock, ticking in the corner. Grant would be back soon, and then they'd all be off, scattering to the four winds—Grant to New York, Zach to Boston, Cade to London.

There was a kind of comfort in knowing that Kyra would be here, where she'd always been, the keeper of the hearth they could all count on to maintain them as a family.

"Why so misty-eyed, baby brother? I thought you liked Stella's coffee."

Cade looked up. Kyra was smiling as she came toward him. She was dressed as he was, in faded jeans and a wool shirt, her leather boots as softly worn and comfortable-looking as his.

"It's chilly this morning," he said, smiling back at her. "Be sure and put on something warmer before you go down to the stables."

His sister sighed. "Words of wisdom from my baby brother," she said. "As always."

Cade smiled and lifted his cheek for her kiss as she made her way past his chair.

"Watch that baby-brother stuff, Squirt. I've got six years on you, in case you've forgotten."

She stood back, put her hands on her hips and looked him over.

"You look like one of the ranch hands," she said.

Cade laughed. "Look who's talking."

His sister grinned. "Yeah. But this *is* a ranch, and I live here. What's your excuse?"

Cade shrugged. "I always dress this way. Hell, these are my working clothes. People get nervous if the guy in charge of bringing in a well sashays around in a suit and tie."

"You're flying to London, dressed like that?"

"Come on, Sis. What is this?"

"Sorry. It's just that I've been looking at my three big brothers all week and thinking it's time you guys settled down."

Cade looked at her blankly, and then he grinned. "Don't tell me you want to marry us off!"

"Having a woman to look after you might be just what you need," Kyra said mildly.

Cade thought of the birthday gift he hadn't had time to unwrap, still awaiting his pleasure in Dumai, and he chuckled.

"Trust me, Squirt," he said. "I've got all the women I need."

"Yeah," his sister said with a little smile as she turned to the sideboard, "I'll just bet you do." She looked at the heaping platters of food, gave a delicate shudder and poured herself a cup of coffee. "I guess somebody'd better tell Stella that she doesn't have to turn out this kind of feed anymore."

"That's your job," Cade said. "You're in charge of Landon House from now on, remember?"

A funny look crept over Kyra's face. "I know," she said slowly. "I still can't believe Dad left the place to me."

"Who else would he have left it to?" Zach said, as he came into the room. "You're the only one of us who gives a damn for this pile of brick." He nodded to Cade, dropped a kiss on the top of Kyra's head, then shot back the cuff of his Harris tweed sports jacket and frowned at his Rolex. "I've got an eleven o'clock flight to Boston. Isn't Grant back from that meeting yet?"

Cade put down his empty cup, rose from his chair and leaned back against the sideboard, his feet crossed at the ankles, hands tucked into the back pockets of his Levi's.

"You're out of uniform, aren't you? I heard you banker types signed a pledge that said you had to go around in pinstripes."

Zach's frown became a grin that softened the ruggedly handsome lines of his face.

"Laugh all you like, pal. Just remember that in a couple of days you'll be cozying up to an English version of me, trying your best to sweet-talk him into investing in your latest search for pie in the sky in—where'd you say you were going this time?"

"The North Sea," Cade said, flashing an answering grin. "And it's not pie in the sky, buddy. It's at least as sure a bet as those investments you tout."

"Yeah?"

"Yeah. And I suspect that if your fancy clients had any idea I could still pin you arm wrestling without breaking a sweat—"

"Still? What do you mean, still? You never beat me, not once."

"Prove it."

"With pleasure. Just let me take off this jacket and—"

"Dammit, what's going on here? Are we kids or what?"

Cade, Zach and Kyra spun around as Grant entered the dining room. He glared at each of them, dropped a manila folder on the table and stalked to the sideboard.

"Grant?" Kyra said. "Are you OK?"

Grant nodded as he poured himself coffee. "Fine."

Not true, thought Cade. Grant's chiseled features, always stern, today seemed to have been carved in granite.

He waited until Grant had taken his first sip of coffee, and then he cleared his throat.

"So," he said, "what did Bayliss want to talk about?"

"Trouble."

"What do you mean? What kind of trouble?"

Grant took the folder from the table. "This kind," he said. He drew out two stacks of papers and handed one to each of his brothers. Kyra waited a moment, and then she turned and walked to the window.

For a while, the only sound in the room was that of rustling paper.

Finally, Cade looked up, his brow furrowed.

"What is this crap?" he said.

"It's just what it looks like. Father bought a small oil company in Dallas—"

"You mean, he bought a disaster." Cade tapped his fingers against the papers he held in his hand. "And then he let it go from bad to worse. It's almost bankrupt."

Zach shook his head. "What are you talking about? This report's got nothing to do with oil. It's about a Hollywood production outfit named Triad, on the verge of going belly up."

"You've each got different reports, drawn up by Bayliss, but the bottom line's the same. It seems Father bought both these companies just before he took ill, and they got lost in the shuffle."

Cade shook his head. "When Gordon Oil goes under, it's going to take a lot of Landon dough with it."

"The same for Triad," Zach said with a scowl. "Landon Enterprises will be lucky if it takes out a dime on a dollar."

Grant's expression was grim. "It seems that Landon went into the two firms to bail them out. Instead, we seem to have helped them get into worse condition."

"What's this 'we' stuff?" Cade said.

"Maybe you've forgotten that, as of yesterday, *we* are Landon Enterprises. And we will be, until we find a buyer."

Cade sighed. "Yeah—and if these babies go under, we'll have a hole in the balance sheet that'll drop the value of the company into the sewer." He looked at Grant. "OK. Tell Bayliss to—"

"Bayliss retired, as of this morning." Grant smiled slightly at the looks on his brothers' faces. "He said he was too old to face another Colorado winter. Seems he bought himself a house in the Virgin Islands somewhere, and he's going to spend the rest of his days on the beach, sipping piña coladas."

"Well, I'll phone Goodwin, then. Bayliss's second in command. He can—"

"Goodwin's got a dozen things on his plate already."

Cade tossed the Gordon Oil report onto the table. "Terrific. Now what do we do?"

"Oh, for heaven's sake!" The men swung around. Kyra was glaring at them, her hands planted firmly on her hips as if she couldn't believe what she'd been hearing. "What's the matter with you guys? Are you stupid, or what?"

"Squirt," Cade said gently, "I know you mean well, but hell, you don't know anything about business, and—"

"A ten-year-old could figure this out!" She looked at Zach. "You're the financial whiz in this family. Surely you could fly out to the coast, take a look at Triad Productions' books and decide what can be done to help it."

"Me? Don't be silly. I've got people waiting for me in Boston. I can't just—"

"And you," she said to Cade. "You're the genius who knows all about oil. And here's this little company, having some kind of problem." Kyra's brows lifted toward her hairline. "Would it be too much to hope that maybe, just maybe, you might be the one to check things out in Dallas?"

"It's out of the question! I've business in London. I can't—"

"She's right," Grant said brusquely. "You guys could get a handle on things faster than anybody else."

There was a moment's silence. Cade and Zach looked at each other, and then Zach threw up his arms in defeat.

"Two days," he snapped, "and not a second more."

Cade blew out his breath. "The same here. Two days, and then... Wait just a minute." He swung toward Grant. "What about you? Don't tell me you're the only one of us who gets to walk away from this mess?"

Grant's expression grew even darker. "It seems some old pal of Father's named him guardian of his kid a couple of years ago."

A smile twitched at the corners of Cade's lips. "Don't tell me," he said.

Grant shrugged. "You pick it, brother mine. Would you rather baby-sit an oil company in Dallas—or a twelve-year-old kid in New York?"

When they finished laughing, the brothers clasped right hands, the way they used to when they were children.

"Here's to the Deadeye Defenders," Cade said solemnly.

"To the Deadeyes," his brothers echoed, and then they grinned and set off in separate directions.

Cade went to the library. He phoned London and postponed his meeting, then settled into a leather armchair and read slowly and carefully through the Gordon Oil report.

When he was done, he breathed a sigh of relief.

Without setting foot in the Gordon Oil office in Dallas, he already knew what the problem was.

Management.

The company's director was running things straight into the ground.

Hank Gordon, the founder, had died a few months ago. Ever since, his daughter had been running the show.

Her name was A.H.

A woman, Cade thought with a shudder of disbelief, heading up an oil company. And if that weren't bad enough, one who used initials instead of a name.

According to the thumbnail sketch Bayliss had provided, A.H. Gordon had spent the last fifteen years of her life in New England. She was a teacher at some fancy girls' school.

Lord. It was a prescription for disaster. Cade could imagine what she was like, a fortyish spinster in tweed, wearing sensible oxfords and wire-rimmed glasses, dishing out orders in a snooty boarding-school accent to a bunch of men who were probably still trying to figure out if old A.H. was male, female or something uncomfortably in between.

Cade hunched over the report again. The more he read, the more he felt like groaning.

It wasn't bad enough she'd lived and taught back East. She'd also taken her degree there, at a college for women. Cade almost laughed. An Eastern college for women was definitely the place to get your education, if you wanted to find out how to deal with a Texas oil crew.

As for what she'd studied—he did laugh, this time.

A.H. Gordon had not one but two degrees, one in business administration and one in psychology.

Either was about as useful in the oil business as teats on a bull.

The business degree might sound good, but Cade had taken a few business courses back in the days when he'd been studying petroleum geology. He could still remember the serious, bearded profs in their tweed jackets with the leather elbow patches, spouting facts and figures to prove that the way to get the most out of your workers was to make them feel a part of the process.

Maybe it worked in a Toyota factory, or on Madison Avenue. But out in an oil field, the way to get the most out of your men was to prove that you were one of them, that you could sweat and strain and wrestle heavy, dangerous equipment the same way they could.

That left A.H. Gordon out.

As for psychology—Cade had taken some of those courses, too, not out of choice, God knew, but because they'd been part of the university's degree requirements.

If A.H. Gordon believed in her subject, then she believed, too, that it was important to worry about everybody's childhood traumas, egos and self-worth.

It was a technique that might work with kids. But if you had to ride herd on a bunch of tough-talking roughnecks, it was doomed to failure.

Cade sighed and settled back in the chair. He stretched out his legs, crossed them at the ankles and scanned the report again, just to make sure he'd gotten the salient facts. Then he slapped it down on the table beside him and laced his fingers together, steepling them below his chin, tapping the tips of his index fingers against his mouth.

A.H., he mused, A.H. Was A for Anne? Alice? Agnes? Cade grinned. Oh, yes, he thought, Agnes. Definitely.

And the H. What was that for? Helen? No, he didn't think so. Harriet? Hannah? Henrietta? Yeah, that was it. Hank Gordon's daughter had been named for her father.

Agnes Henrietta Gordon. That was the woman's name. He could feel it in his bones.

To think he'd expected to spend two whole days sorting things out in Dallas. An hour right here had done the job. All he needed to do was remove A.H. Gordon from the top spot at Gordon Oil and replace her with someone who could handle the job.

He would do it tactfully, if he could. But if he couldn't...

He reached for the telephone, ran his finger down the list of numbers programmed into it, found the one he wanted and hit the button. Minutes later, he was ticketed on the next flight to Dallas. Then he trotted up the stairs to his room and tugged his leather carryon from the wardrobe closet.

He felt a twinge of regret for A.H. Gordon. The job heading up Gordon Oil must have fallen on her shoulders after her father's death. By now, she was probably close to panic, lost and alone in a man's world. In fact, she was probably eager to step aside. She just didn't know how to do it gracefully—but he'd show her.

Cade pulled open the bureau drawers and began tossing shirts and undershorts into the carryon. And if, by some remote possibility, she wasn't quite ready to relinquish control of the company, he'd just have to be brutally frank.

"A.H.," he'd say, clapping her on her overstuffed, tweedy back, "you're not helping Gordon Oil reach its full potential."

Cade grinned as he strode into the connecting bathroom and gathered his toiletries. A psych major ought to appreciate that approach. Then he'd appoint someone to take her place—one of his own men, perhaps, or someone whose ability caught his eye at Gordon's—and climb on the first plane leaving Dallas for London.

Or maybe he'd go to England the long way, with a stopover in Dumai first, where that beautiful, gift-wrapped package still waited for him. He smiled as he conjured up an image of heavily lashed eyes, a soft mouth and a lush body.

What had her name been? Leilia. A sexy name for a sexy woman, one who was as lovely as she was eager to come to sweet, exciting life in a man's arms.

He wondered what such a woman would make of an A.H. Gordon.

It might be simpler to convince a poodle and a fox terrier that they were related, he thought, and chuckled.

Whistling softly between his teeth, he zipped the carryon shut, stepped briskly into the hall and shut the bedroom door after him.

CHAPTER TWO

ANGELICA Gordon was not a happy woman.

She had creditors breathing down her neck, a drilling crew threatening to strike and so many bills to pay that she'd given up looking at her morning mail.

Even worse, she had a meeting in two hours with a hatchet man for Landon Enterprises.

No, she thought as she yanked a black linen dress from her wardrobe closet and eyed it critically, no, she was not happy at all.

Angelica frowned, held the dress under her chin and glared at herself in the mirror.

The idea was to look like an executive, not the chief mourner at a funeral. She tossed the dress on the bed, where it joined a small but growing pile of discards.

Why hadn't they given her more warning? It was unconscionable, announcing a visit only hours in advance. Suppose she'd had a conflicting appointment that couldn't be canceled?

Angelica blew an errant copper curl off her forehead. That was probably the whole point of doing it this way, she thought grimly. The fax Emily had read her over the phone spoke of "urgent business," but anyone who knew anything about business strategy would realize that the only business that was urgent was reminding her that Landon Enterprises could make her jump through hoops any time it wanted.

Not that she needed reminding. Landon owned her, lock, stock and barrel. They had the right to do virtually anything they chose—and she suspected that what they chose was to remove her as head of Gordon Oil.

Well, she wasn't going to make it easy for them. She'd tried her hardest to make this work. Surely, they'd understand....

Angelica groaned softly and sat down on the edge of the bed. The only thing Landon would understand was Gordon's downward spiral.

Maybe her friends back east had been right all along.

Jack Brenner, who taught mathematics at Miss Palmer's and with whom she'd shared an occasional meal or movie, had been blunt.

"You're not superwoman! Just because your father left you a run-down business doesn't mean you have to give up your life to go save it."

Angelica had tried to explain that Gordon Oil would be a challenge.

"It's a chance to really use my skills," she'd said.

"You're using them," Jack had insisted, "as careers adviser at the academy. You're good at your job, and you like it."

"I do like it—but this field wasn't my first choice. I have a degree in business, too, remember? I *always* wanted a career at Gordon Oil. I've got ideas for its growth, and plans—"

"What about living in Texas? How are you going to handle that?"

Angelica had smiled. "Texas *is* part of the United States, Jack."

"But you've lived here most of your life."

"Yes, almost fifteen years. I moved here with my mother after my parents divorced—but where I've lived isn't the point! Don't you see? My father left me his company—"

"Right," Jack had said grimly. "He left it to you. He didn't say anything about wanting you to run it."

That was true, but it only made the need to prove herself as director of Gordon Oil more appealing. Angelica had quit Miss Palmer's, packed her things and moved back to the city where she'd been born.

Within weeks, she suspected she'd made a mistake.

The oil business seemed to be run by Hank Gordon clones. Men were men, women were second-class citizens—and old Hank had been an asshole to have left his company to his daughter.

Except it turned out Hank hadn't really done that at all. Her father's will had been as disorganized as his books. Within weeks of arriving in Dallas, Angelica had learned he'd actually sold the company to the enormous Landon conglomerate a couple of months before his death.

But Landon's hadn't so much as contacted her. After a while, Angelica started to feel as if the company really was hers. She'd settled in at the tiny office, traveled out to the scattered drilling sites . . .

And found disaster. Hank Gordon had known how to find oil but not how to run a business. He'd still been using management policies that dated to the days when Texas was part of the wild West!

With a weary sigh, Angelica got to her feet, made her way to the bathroom and stepped into the shower. A few weeks ago, she'd dutifully mailed a quarterly report to Landon's main office. It showed that Gordon's debts had grown larger, its income smaller, its work crews less productive, and all since she'd taken over.

Angelica shut off the water, stepped onto the bath mat and toweled herself dry. Not that it was her fault. Change was never easy, especially when you were dealing with a bunch of men who thought the world had been a better place when wagon trains were still rolling across the plains.

She had to make the Landon rep understand what had happened here, that she'd been defeated not by her lack of ability but by the enormity of the job that needed doing. After all, this man would speak her language. He'd understand flow charts and team leadership and employee-generated goals, all the things that were needed to make a success of Gordon Oil.

Her spirits lifted. She leaned forward and wiped the foggy mirror with the heel of her hand. Her face peered back at her, a pale oval pierced by wide-spaced green eyes.

"Approach this meeting positively," she said crisply, "and it will be a success!"

Quickly, she blew her hair dry, determinedly ignoring the curling tendrils that sprang up as quickly as she brushed them flat. Her hair was impossible, both in color and texture. She'd tried everything to tame it over the years, from shearing it off with a pair of scissors when she was twelve to dyeing it a shade euphemistically called Mahogany Glory her freshman year at college.

Nothing worked. Cutting it short only meant she couldn't subdue the curls with barrettes or clips, and darkening the color had made the smattering of freckles across the bridge of her small, straight nose seem to leap off her face.

Angelica's spirits dipped just a little. This was not the hair of an efficient executive, she thought, staring at her reflection. Already, bright copper curls were springing up around her face and falling in a wild tumble over her shoulders.

How could a woman with two degrees, a serious nature and the responsibility of running a company have been given hair like this?

With a sigh, she scooped the curls from her face and secured them at the nape of her neck with a coated rubber band. Then, head high, she marched into the bedroom.

What did her hair matter? She had a presentation to make to the man from Landon's, one that would convince him to give her more time to drag Gordon Oil into the modern world, she was sure of it.

Almost sure, she amended, and sighed.

She stepped into a brown wool skirt, slipped on a white blouse, buttoned it to the Peter Pan collar and topped it with an oatmeal tweed jacket. She hesitated only over the shoes. She was tall for a woman, five foot eight in her stocking feet. Even in her sensible pumps, she might end up taller than her visitor.

Would he find that intimidating?

She'd wear flats and play it safe. The last thing she wanted to do was get on the Landon rep's bad side.

At last, she turned and looked at herself in the mirror.

Efficient, she thought, nodding her head. Very efficient.

Angelica glanced at the clock, rolled her eyes and snatched her briefcase from the top of the bureau. She hurried through the little house that had been her father's, out the front door to her small, late-model sedan parked at the curb.

A gentle breeze played at her hair, helping to ease the wisps of copper that were already bouncing lightly against her forehead and cheeks. Unconsciously, she stuck out her bottom lip and blew the stray curls back.

"OK, Landon Enterprises," she said as she got behind the wheel, "I'm ready!"

So armed, Angelica Gordon carefully checked both her side and rearview mirrors, flicked on her signal light and pulled out into the street.

At noon, Angelica cleared her desk and gave strict instructions to Emily, her secretary and all-purpose gofer. The representative was due in an hour. Emily was to greet him, seat him in the one nonrickety chair in the waiting room, then immediately inform Angelica of his arrival.

"Then bring us some coffee, please, Emily, if you don't mind. I know I normally get my own—you know how I feel about equality in the workplace, but—"

"It's not a problem, A.H."

"Thank you. And, oh—be sure and hold all my calls."

By two, Angelica was pacing her tiny office, wearing furrows in the already threadbare carpet.

At two-thirty, she stepped into the anteroom and looked at Emily.

"Are you sure the fax said he would be here at one?"

Emily shrugged. "That's what it said, all right. It took two tries for it to come through—the phone company cut off service in the middle but I went out to the booth on the corner, called the business office and explained—"

"—that their check was in the mail," Angelica said impatiently. "But the fax was specific, is that correct? We did get a message saying he was coming in today on the flight from Denver?"

"Uh-huh. And before you ask, I already checked with the airport. The flight came in on time."

Angelica's green eyes narrowed just a little. "Did it?"

"Maybe his taxi's stuck in traffic."

And maybe she was being taught her place in the scheme of things, Angelica thought, but she forced the idea out of her mind.

It was important to greet the man in a positive frame of mind.

"You're right," she said. "Traffic from the airport can be awful. We'll just wait."

There was no sense in wasting even more of the day than she already had. With a sigh, she opened the bottom drawer of her desk, took out the letters, bills and odds and ends she'd dumped into it and spread them across her blotter.

Maybe if she kept busy working, time would pass more quickly. She could clear the desk again easily enough once Emily announced her visitor's arrival.

At three, Angelica shoved back her chair. So much for being treated with dignity—and so much for hoping Landon Enterprises would agree to give her more time to prove herself. She was going to be fired, that was obvious, but first she was going to have a ration of crow shoved down her throat.

She stood up and marched to the door.

"When the gentleman finally arrives," she told Emily in clipped tones, "tell him I'm busy. Sit him down, hand him today's paper and let him wait ten or fifteen minutes before you ring me."

Emily's brows lifted. "You sure you want me to do that?"

"It's a simple reverse power play, Emily. The man is establishing his dominance, so I'll have to make it clear that I don't see myself in a subordinate role." Her smile was tight. "It's not a problem, I assure you."

At four, Angelica stabbed the button on her intercom, folded her hands on her desk blotter and waited.

Emily came hurrying into the office. "A.H.," she said, "I was just going to—"

"I know it's pointless to let myself get angry," Angelica said, very, very calmly, "especially since I know he may be doing this to try and unnerve me, but—"

"A.H., listen—"

"—but," Angelica said, shoving back her chair and rising to her feet, "who in hell does this human hatchet think he is?"

"Oh, A.H., please, don't say such things. You—"

"I know. I know." Angelica took a deep breath and looked at the ceiling. "I should not let this upset me. I should consider what his motives might be." Her eyes snapped to Emily's. "How dare he?" she asked. "Of course, I'm not surprised. Anyone who would work for an outfit like Landon's can't care too much about decency or morality. Those people are sharks, Emily, they're hyenas who smell blood and come hurrying in for the kill."

Emily groaned softly. "A.H.—"

"If and when the weasel gets here, tell him I got tired of waiting and I've left for the day."

"No! A.H.—"

"I know you think I ought to wait for the man, Emily, but it's important I not let those people get away with this. If they think I'm going to let them intimidate me—"

"I can't imagine that anyone could do that, Miss Gordon," a deep voice said.

Angelica spun around. There was a man in the doorway. He had a square jaw, a dimpled chin and a nose that was just enough off-center to give his incredibly handsome face interest. He was tall, broad-shouldered, impeccably dressed in a pale gray suit, white shirt and blue and red striped tie—a picture of custom-tailored elegance, forever spoiled by the mirror-bright black boots peeping out from under his trouser cuffs.

"I beg your pardon," she said coldly. "This is a private office. If you have business here—"

"Just what, pray tell, *is* a human hatchet, Miss Gordon?" A smile so arrogant it bordered on insult tilted the corner of his mouth. "It's an interesting description but I'm afraid I can't quite get the image."

Angelica flushed but her gaze didn't waver. "You've been eavesdropping as well as trespassing."

The man shrugged lazily. "Your door was open. If you meant your remarks to be private—"

"No matter what you're selling, I'm not interested."

"A.H.," Emily begged, "please—"

"Do I look like a salesman, Miss Gordon?"

Angelica looked at him. No, she thought, he did not. He looked—he looked like a pirate in twentieth-century clothing, like a Viking who'd stepped into the wrong time and place.

"How can you not be interested in what I'm selling if you don't know what it is?"

"I thought you said you weren't..." Angelica puffed out her breath. "Look, I'll give you one more chance. Are you going to leave on your own, or—"

"Or?" His voice was soft, but somehow there was a world of menace in the single word.

"A.H.," Emily said, "listen to me!"

"Yes, A.H." The man laughed, his teeth very white against his tanned skin. "She's right, you know. You really should listen to her."

He leaned away from the door frame and started slowly toward Angelica. His lazy posture had been deceptive, she thought wildly; he moved with the easy grace and purpose of a jungle cat, and there was a sudden hard look in his eyes that made her want to take a hurried step back.

But she didn't.

"Emily," she said in what she hoped was a firm tone, "call security. Tell them—"

"Who're you kidding, Miss Gordon?" He stopped in the center of the room, his eyes narrowing as they met hers. "You don't have security. You probably don't even have somebody to come in and sweep the floors."

"The police, then." Angelica forced her eyes to stay locked with his. "Emily, dammit, what are you waiting for? If this—this person thinks he can muscle his way in here—"

"Are you sure your phone is working, Miss Gordon?" His voice was bemused, almost gentle. "Perhaps you should try to get a dial tone before you make any more threats."

"Did you do something to the phone lines?" Angelica swung toward her secretary. "Emily, why are you standing there? Didn't you hear me? Go call the—"

"For heaven's sake," Emily hissed, her round face drained of all color, "I've been trying and trying to tell you, A.H.! This man isn't a salesman. He—"

"Emily! What's wrong with you? I don't care who he is. I want you to—"

"He's—he's Landon!"

Silence seemed to descend on the little room. Angelica stared at her secretary.

"He's what?" she whispered.

Emily threw her hands in the air. "He's the man you've been waiting for!"

Slowly, Angelica turned and looked at the stranger. The smile was on his lips again, this time not just arrogant but smug.

"Have you been waiting for me, sugar?" he purred. "How sweet."

Crimson slashes appeared on Angelica's high cheekbones.

"You're from Landon?" she said in disbelief.

Emily scurried past the man and out the door, closing it softly behind her.

"No," he said, "I'm not."

He moved forward again, until he was standing beside Angelica. She had to tilt her head to look at him.

I could have worn heels after all, she thought foolishly, and the patches of crimson rimming her cheeks deepened.

"But—but Emily said—"

Cade laughed and strolled past her to her desk, heaped with what were obviously unpaid—hell, unopened—bills.

"I'm not *from* Landon," he said, quite pleasantly, "I *am* Landon. Cade Landon, to be precise, of the Landon sharks—or was it hyenas?"

Oh, the look on her face was wonderful. Wonderful! He might as well have said he was the devil incarnate.

Miss A.H. Gordon knew exactly what would happen next, and so did he. In just a little while, this priggish female in the funny tweed suit would be out on her ass.

But he wasn't ready to drop that news on her quite yet, Cade thought, trailing a finger over the stack of unanswered letters that overflowed her correspondence tray. There was too much pleasure in drawing things out. It was the least he owed her, considering the way his day—thanks to her—had gone so far.

A traffic jam had kept him from reaching the airport in Denver in time to make his flight, and he'd had to charter a private plane. He'd already had the office fax Dallas word of his impending visit; now, he'd tried to phone and tell them of his change of plans but he'd found the number busy, then out of service.

"That's impossible," he'd told the operator. "It's a business number. It can't be out of service."

"Actually, sir," the disembodied female voice had said, "the number's been disconnected."

Cade had slammed down the phone, his expression grim, willing to bet everything he owned that the number had been disconnected for nonpayment of bills.

Thunderstorms midway between Denver and Dallas had delayed his arrival time again, but the final straw had come when he'd reached the airport and discovered that no one on this end had arranged for the transportation he'd requested in his fax.

By the time he'd made his own arrangements for a rental car and driven through a maze of streets to get to this godforsaken part of the city, his disposition had been decidedly unpleasant. Still, he'd been glad when he saw the Gordon Oil sign, even though it hung outside what looked like a shack.

Cade had come through the door into a cramped anteroom overflowing with file cabinets.

"Landon," he'd said brusquely. "I'm here to see A.H. Gordon."

The receptionist had led him to a chair that creaked alarmingly and stabbed a newspaper he didn't want to read into his hands. Miss Gordon was too busy to see him just yet, she said, and looked as if she'd rather have bitten her tongue off than have said the words. He was to make himself comfortable and wait.

Cade had done that until his rising blood pressure threatened to blow the top of his head off. Then he'd shot to his feet and stalked to the woman's desk.

"Listen, lady," he'd said, "you go on in and tell your boss that Cade Landon wants to see her, and pronto."

The woman's eyes had gone round like saucers. "You mean, your *name* is Landon?" she'd squeaked.

"That's right. And I'm not going to sit out here, cooling my heels, another minute."

Just then, the intercom had buzzed. The woman had escaped past him, thrown open the door to A.H.

Gordon's office—and it had been all fun and games from there, Cade thought with a little smile.

"What are you smiling at?"

Cade's brows rose in surprise. He turned around. The Gordon woman was staring at him, her oval face tilted up to his, her expression one of absolute defiance.

"There's nothing amusing in any of this, Mr. Landon. And I don't like you handling my things."

"Your things?" he said. "No, Miss Gordon, you've got that wrong. I own this place, not you."

"You don't own correspondence addressed to me," Angelica said, although she had no idea if that were true or not. She folded her arms over her chest. "And if you're waiting for me to apologize—well, I suppose I'm sorry you overheard the things I said." Her small, resolute chin rose even higher. "But if you hadn't eavesdropped, you wouldn't have heard any of it."

Well, well, well, Cade thought. This was going to be amusing. The woman was a tiger, he had to give her that much. Her tone was almost as frosty as her eyes.

He frowned. Were her eyes really green? Yes, they were. He wasn't sure he'd seen a color quite like it before, something between the color of emeralds and the deep green of an Arctic sea.

His gaze flickered over her face. The green went well with her cloud of bright copper hair. She had pulled it back in some sort of ugly arrangement that made her skin look as if it were too tight for the bones of her face, but curls were escaping in all directions. Wisps of copper danced against her temples and forehead; a feathery trail hung down the long column of her throat and brushed the collar of her tweed jacket.

It was an odd and incongruous combination, the tweed and the coppery strands of hair. They looked soft as silk. Were they? Would they curl around his finger if he put out his hand and...

Cade jammed his hands into his trouser pockets and frowned. What did the woman's hair have to do with anything? This sharp-tongued bitch had been running Gordon's into the ground—but what else could anyone have expected? Not only was she a woman in a man's world, a refugee from an intellectual ivy-covered tower, she was also a child. It had been instantly obvious that she wasn't middle-aged, as he'd expected her to be, but now, with her standing this close, he could see that she couldn't even be thirty!

In fact, if he hadn't known she was a university graduate, he'd have pegged her at eighteen, nineteen at the most. She had an untouched look about her, an un-awakened look, and Cade wondered, all at once, how it would feel to be the man who turned the ice in those green eyes to fire, who made that smug, rosebud mouth soften with passion...

Jesus! This was what came of not having had breakfast or lunch, of missing planes and enduring thunderstorms and dealing with car rental clerks who never seemed to have the make or model you really wanted.

Enough, he thought, and he looked straight at A.H. Gordon.

"You're fired," he said coldly. "I'll give you the rest of the day to pack your things and vacate this office. My people will cut you a check. Two months' severance pay, and—"

"No!" Angelica's voice trembled. This wasn't the way this meeting was to have gone! What of her presentation? Her charts? "No," she repeated. She took a step toward him, her face flushed, her hands balled into fists at her sides. "You can't fire me this way! You—"

He laughed. "Of course I can. Please, Miss Gordon, don't waste my time. Pack your things and get out."

"I demand a meeting with Charles Landon. Or with Victor Bayliss. He's Charles Landon's righthand man, isn't he? Well, I want to talk with him. He'll understand my situation."

Cade's smile turned grim. "You're out of touch, Miss Gordon. My father is dead and Bayliss has retired. I'm the one you have to answer to now."

"That's ridiculous!" Angelica frowned. "I mean, I'm sorry about your father, but—"

"Thank you for your commiseration," he said coldly. "I'm touched. Deeply. But I still want you out of here today."

Angelica drew herself up. "Listen here, Mr. Landon! This company was my father's! Do you have any idea—"

"OK, you've got a point there."

"You mean—"

"I can see where you might feel entitled to—let's say six months' severance pay. After all, as you point out, you did have a very personal connection to this place."

"You—you bastard!"

Cade's brows lifted. "Such language, A.H. I'm stunned."

"You—you—"

He laughed. "Next time, sweetheart, think twice before you decide to kick somebody out of your office."

"I refuse to believe you have the authority to do this!" Angelica slapped her hands on her hips. "I'm not packing and I'm not vacating my office and it'll take more than the likes of you to make me!"

She gasped as Cade reached out and caught hold of her shoulders.

"You want proof that I'm in authority here, lady?" His eyes—blue, she thought incongruously, so blue they were almost bottomless pools—glinted dangerously as he pulled her into his arms. "Well, then," he growled, "here it is!"

Angelica cried out and tried to turn her head away, but he was too quick and too strong. His mouth came down on hers, his lips harsh and cool, his hands slipping to her face and holding it fast.

"Don't," she gasped, twisting hard against him, but he only laughed.

"What's the matter, A.H.? Haven't you ever been kissed before?"

"Bastard," she hissed, just before his mouth descended on hers...

...And, suddenly, Angelica felt a flame flicker to life deep within her. She made a little sound, not quite a whimper and not quite a moan, and Cade answered with a sound from deep in his throat. His arms tightened around her; his mouth opened hungrily over hers and she rose on her toes, her arms closed around his neck and she lifted herself to him, heart racing...

Cade thrust her from him and stared at her, his eyes blurred. What in hell had just happened? Anger, he thought, that was it. Yeah. Anger could be one hell of an aphrodisiac.

"You see?" he said. His voice was cool—a miracle, he thought, considering that every muscle in his body felt knot-hard. "I am definitely in charge here, Miss Gordon, whether you want to admit it or not. And, since I am, I'll be generous." He smiled tightly and leaned back against the desk, arms folded over his chest. "A year's pay, A.H., and you have until tomorrow to get out."

Angelica looked at him. She was trembling and it seemed difficult to draw enough air into her lungs—but that was understandable, given what she'd been through in the past few minutes.

This smug, insolent, overbearing cowboy whose shoe size was probably greater than his IQ had barged into her office, insulted her, bullied her and treated her with a macho contempt so unbelievable that she'd come close to being immobilized—for surely that was the only reason he'd been able to get away with kissing her.

She smiled, although it took enormous effort.

"That is indeed generous, Mr. Landon," she said. "Very generous." Her smile grew dazzling. "But I keep trying to tell you, you can't fire me."

He sighed. "A.H.," he said wearily, "aren't you tired of this little game?"

Angelica cocked her head. "Don't you know about the agreement?"

Cade frowned. "What agreement?"

She smiled again, and the lie tripped off her lips as if it were the greatest truth the world had ever heard.

"Why, the one that grants me the right to remain head of Gordon Oil for so long as I wish," she said. She watched his handsome face whiten and it was all she could do to keep from laughing. "Which pretty much means," she said sweetly, "that I'm going to stay on forever."

CHAPTER THREE

THERE were three telephones in Cade's suite, one in each of the two bedrooms and one in the sitting room. In the short time since he'd checked into the elegant hotel, he'd come to hate them all.

He knew it was crazy to feel anger for lumps of white plastic. It was just that the damned things sat there, silent and smug, almost as smug as A.H. Gordon had looked when she'd dropped her bombshell on him a couple of hours ago.

Cade muttered a short, sharp oath, yanked off his tie and tossed it after his already discarded jacket.

"Dammit, Grant," he said as he undid the button on his shirt, "what's taking you so long?"

He'd called New York hours ago. Surely Grant had been able to check the Gordon contract by now.

Not that there was much point to it. A clause granting Hank Gordon's daughter control of Gordon Oil could exist nowhere but in the woman's scheming brain. Charles Landon might have been out of touch with things at the end, but he'd sooner have made a chimpanzee head of the company than her. Cade had told her as much—after he'd finished laughing.

A.H. Gordon had just stood there, her green eyes growing even colder, not backing down an inch, and Cade's laughter had given way to anger. If only she were only a man, he'd thought, his fists clenching.

But she wasn't. She was a woman and, all at once, he'd wanted nothing so badly as to take her in his arms and kiss her until she remembered that.

Without another word, he'd walked out of her office, climbed into his rental car and driven to this hotel, where the desk clerk had taken one look at his face and said

44

yes, certainly, there was a suite available even without a reservation.

And then he'd telephoned Grant—who should damned well have called back by now.

Cade leveled another furious look at the telephone.

"Ring," he said through his teeth, "or so help me, I'll pull you out of the wall by your cord and—"

The phone rang. He made a diving grab for it and jammed the receiver against his ear.

"It's about time," he snarled.

"'Hello, Grant,'" Grant said mildly. "'Thanks for walking out on your dinner date and getting back to me so quickly.'"

Cade's eyes narrowed. "Dinner?" he said. "What in hell is dinner? Does it have anything to do with eating? It's been so long since I had a meal that I can't be certain."

His brother sighed. "It's past eight here, Cade. I had to contact Colorado, have them fax me a copy of the contract and—"

"And?"

"And, just as you figured, it's a standard buy-out agreement."

Cade sat down on the sofa. "Meaning, there's no reference to Hank Gordon's daughter running the show."

"Exactly."

A smile eased across Cade's mouth. "Goodbye, A.H. Gordon," he said softly.

"It's Angelica."

"What?"

"Her name. It's Angelica. I don't know what the middle initial is for, but—"

"Angelica?" Cade laughed. "Sorry, pal. You'll have to try again. Katherine the Shrew, maybe, but—"

"I caught Bayliss as he was cleaning out his office and I asked him if he could think of any other info on the deal. He couldn't—but he remembered her given name."

Cade shook his head. "Man, if ever there was a misnomer, that's it. There are lots of things I'd call this broad, but Angelica is definitely not one of them."

"Tell me again what she said about the agreement that supposedly puts her in charge."

"Grant," Cade said patiently, "I appreciate your wanting to make sure there are no loose ends, but you've just told me, it was a standard buy-out deal. Now, it's late, and I wasn't kidding when I said I haven't eaten in—"

"Did she actually claim it was part of the contract?"

"No! And you just said it wasn't, so what's the point of—"

"Did she mention having an addendum stashed somewhere?"

"Dammit, Grant, I'd have told you if—"

"Then the only thing left is a verbal agreement."

"Hey, wait a minute! How'd we skip past the part where she's lying through her teeth?"

"Courts everywhere have held that a verbal contract's as legal as a written one—but surely you're aware of that."

"Sure. I've gone into a dozen deals on nothing more substantial than a 'yes' and a handshake, but—" Warning bells started going off in Cade's head. "Is that what you think she's going to claim? That there was an unwritten agreement between the principals?"

"Anything's possible, Cade. She's bound to know something about contract law—she studied business administration, didn't she?"

All at once, the long day seemed to catch up. Cade switched the phone to his other ear and closed his eyes.

"So, what are you telling me?"

Grant sighed. "Only that Angelica Gordon may be able to tie us in legal knots for months."

"Listen, whatever she claims, nobody will believe her. Nobody who knew Charles Landon, anyway."

"You're talking about opinion, Cade. I'm talking about law. Who knows what a judge would believe? Bayliss said the old man wasn't himself at the end, remember? He said—"

"To hell with Bayliss!" Cade shot to his feet, his face dark with anger. "And to hell with Angelica Gordon! She's lying."

"Yes. I'm sure she is, but—"

"She's lying, and I'll prove it!"

Grant sighed. "How?"

"I don't know how." Cade stalked across the room, the telephone cord trailing after him like a snake. "But I'll find a way. Dammit, I'm not going to let this—this uptight, frigid broad keep us dancing around like fools while she plays her little game."

"Uptight, frigid broad, huh?" Grant chuckled. "An interesting description, if ever I heard one."

"It's accurate, and it's probably why she's getting such a kick out of insisting on trying to do a man's job."

"Careful," Grant said gently. "I know you've been off in the wilds of Arabia the past few months, but we've got sex discrimination laws to contend with in this part of the world."

"How about stupidity laws?" Cade growled. "The woman's too brainless to know the first thing about how to run that company."

Grant's laughter sounded hollow. "She's not brainless if she's figured out a way to sabotage Landon Enterprises."

"She wants Gordon Oil, Grant, and it's obvious she'll do anything she has to do to get it." Cade thrust his hand into his sun-streaked hair. "I could toss her over my shoulder, carry her off to a cabin in the Pecos and keep her there until she tells me the truth," he said grimly.

"That might be going a little far, don't you think?"

Suddenly, Cade felt the heat of a blazing hearth. Angelica Gordon was in his arms. Her fiery copper hair streamed over her naked shoulders; her soft, rosebud mouth was swollen from his kisses and her emerald eyes were blurred with desire....

"Damn."

"Cade? What's the matter?"

Cade gave a little laugh. "Nothing. I just need to put some food in my belly before my brain cells stop functioning altogether."

"Look, we'll come up with some kind of game plan."

"We don't need one! She can claim what she likes, but without proof—"

"A court would have to decide what constitutes proof."

"Yeah," Cade said. There was a dull throbbing pain at the base of his skull. He wrapped his hand around the back of his neck and massaged the taut muscles. "OK, here's what we do. Get in touch with Bayliss again. Lean on him a little; make sure he's remembered everything he can. Check the files. Maybe there's a memo we missed."

"Will do."

"How long until I hear from you?"

He could almost see Grant shrug. "I don't know. A couple of days, maybe."

So much for that little stopover in Dumai, Cade thought, and the throbbing pain in his head intensified.

"OK," he said. "Meanwhile, I'll see what I can get out of the Gordon woman."

"Be careful, Cade. Be subtle. We don't want to give her any ideas."

Cade gave a bark of laughter. "Trust me, pal. She's got enough ideas for both of us."

His brother chuckled. "She's as bad as that, huh?"

"Imagine a cross between Lizzie Borden and a bulldog, and you've got the picture."

"Well, do the best you can. If you can find out whether she's playing us along or she's really got something—"

"She's got nothing. You and I both know it."

"Just don't lose your cool."

"No," Cade said, "no, I won't."

"Whatever's she's up to, we can handle it."

Cade nodded as he hung up the phone. Of course, they could handle it. Angelica Gordon might be fast on her feet, she might be clever, but if she really thought she could pull a fast one on the Landons, she was in for an unpleasant surprise.

He walked to the window and looked out. Night had fallen over Dallas; the city's skyline was brightly lit but the glass under his palms was cool.

The Gordon woman's skin had felt like that, cool under his touch, but there'd been a hint of heat lying just underneath, a sense that hidden deep within her, an ember waited for the breath of life...

Cade swore. He swung away from the window, went to the phone and dialed.

"Room service?" he said briskly. "I want a steak, medium rare, a green salad and a baked potato with sour cream. Coffee—a large pot. And a double slice of apple pie. And make it as quick as you can, will you?" He gave a self-deprecating laugh. "I'm desperate."

He hung up the phone, stripped off his shirt and made his way into the tiled bathroom. A shower, a decent meal and a good night's sleep would put him back on his feet.

Tomorrow, he'd confront A.H. Gordon.

A tight smile curled across his mouth as he kicked off his shoes and stepped out of his trousers.

Correction. Tomorrow he'd confront Angelica Gordon.

Weren't there primitive peoples who believed your enemy gained strength by knowing your real name?

"Angelica," Cade said softly, "Miss Angelica Gordon."

Still smiling, he stepped into the shower.

Angelica pulled her Ford Escort to the curb, stepped out onto the pavement and started along the narrow, uneven path that led to her office. Halfway there, she stopped, puffed out her breath and hurried back to the car.

She'd forgotten to lock it, something that was not a wise move in this part of town, but then, she was in one hell of a rush this morning.

Emily looked up as she came into the office.

"Good morning," Emily said, and smiled hesitantly as if to test whether or not this was, in fact, a good morning.

Angelica took a breath and forced a smile to her lips.

"Good morning, Emily."

"Are you, uh, are you OK?"

"Why wouldn't I be?" Angelica said. She scooped her mail off her secretary's desk and headed for her office. "I don't want to be disturbed for an hour or so, please. If anyone calls, take a message."

"Even if it's Mr. Landon?"

"Especially if it's Mr. Landon. If he phones, tell him I'm out."

Angelica slammed her office door, tossed her mail on her desk and went to the bookcase where her old college textbooks stood jammed among the dog-eared volumes on oil that had been her father's.

Frowning, she squatted and peered at the spines.

Yesterday, angry beyond measure at the insufferably rude, impossibly boorish, disgustingly macho Cade Landon, she'd tossed out a lie that had, for the moment, rocked him back on his custom-made boots.

What a pleasure it had been to see him turn pale beneath that artful suntan—achieved, no doubt, at the same health club where he'd gained all those muscles, for it was obvious that he was no more a cowboy than she was.

Not that that improved his stock, Angelica thought grimly. If there was anything worse than a born-and-bred cowboy, it was a phony who pretended to be one.

Oh, there'd been so many reasons it had given her pleasure to drop that lie on the bastard! Born of desperation, it had only been something to give him a night's worth of bad dreams—until this morning, when she'd suddenly remembered something from that long-ago business law course.

Damn! Where was that book hiding?

Angelica got to her feet, brushed the dust from her hands and looked around the room. There were a couple of shelves of her father's books on the wall over her desk. Could *An Introduction to Business Law* have ended up there? Maybe. There was a book way up at the top that looked vaguely familiar.

Angelica dragged her chair back and maneuvered it into position under the shelves. Her skirt—wool, gray and long—would be restrictive, and she quickly hiked it above her knees. She eyed the shelves one last time. Cobwebs, she thought with a little shudder, and she peeled off her gray tweed jacket and dropped it on the desk.

The chair swayed delicately when she stepped on it. She hesitated. Swivel chairs, especially old, unsteady ones, were not made for climbing, but if she were careful...

Angelica clutched the chair back, then straightened slowly and peered at the shelves. Yes, that was the book, all right, on the top shelf at the very end.

Gingerly, she reached toward it. Her sweater scooted up, baring her midriff. Her skirt did the same as it rode up her thighs, but she concentrated on the book, determinedly ignoring the ominous tilt of the chair.

Success! Her fingers closed around the thick volume. Angelica drew it to her and opened to the index.

"Contracts," she murmured, her forefinger skimming the listing, "contracts, legal; contracts, verbal—"

She flipped to the page indicated, scanned it and began to smile.

Her early-morning revelation had been right on the mark! Two parties could, indeed, enter into a verbal

commitment—a commitment that was as binding as any
signed document.

Dust motes burst into the air like champagne bubbles
as she slammed the book shut.

"Gotcha, Mr. Almighty Landon," she whispered
gleefully. Still smiling, she stretched to cram the book
back on the shelf. "Oh, yes, I've got you by the—"

"What in hell do you think you're doing?"

The voice—angry, male and completely unexpected—
seemed to bounce off the walls. Angelica started, gave
a muffled cry—and her feet and the chair parted
company.

Strong, masculine arms closed about her, catching her
as she fell. Heart thumping, she clasped a pair of hard-
muscled shoulders encased in a wool suit jacket, inhaled
a whiff of soap and angry male, and stared into Cade
Landon's icy blue eyes.

"Are you crazy?" he said, in a tone that made it clear
he didn't need or expect an answer. "You don't climb
on swivel chairs, lady, you sit on them!"

"I—I needed to get something from that shelf.
And—"

"And you did it the first damned fool way that came
into your head!"

"Look, I would never have fallen if you hadn't come
barging in and—and—"

"You're damned lucky I did. Otherwise, you'd
probably have broken your fool neck!"

"Don't be ridiculous. You're the reason I—I—"

All at once, Angelica became painfully aware of how
Cade was holding her. He'd caught her in his up-
stretched arms, which meant that she was looking down
at him, that her breasts were almost on a level with his
face and that her belly was pressed tightly against his
muscular chest.

Something deep within her seemed to stretch feathery
wings. She swallowed, then cleared her throat.

"Put me down, please," she said.

"It surely doesn't take two college degrees to know that human beings aren't meant to scramble around like monkeys!"

"Did you hear me, Mr. Landon? Please put me down."

Cade shifted Angelica's weight in his arms. She was lighter than he'd have thought she'd be, and much softer. When he'd kissed her yesterday, there'd been too much woolly tweed between them. Now, thanks to her hiked-up skirt and too-short sweater, he could feel cool inches of smooth, feminine skin.

"No wonder you can't run this place," he said, his tone growing harsher. "Why, you haven't got the sense of a—"

"Don't lecture me!"

"Somebody should have lectured you, lady, and they should have done it a long time ago."

"Dammit," Angelica said. She began to struggle to free herself from Cade's unwanted embrace. "You are the most—"

The angry words caught in her throat. Her efforts to escape had somehow only made his arms close more tightly around her. Now they were pressed together like lovers—and every hard, heated inch of his well-muscled body suggested that he was unquestionably a more than proficient lover.

Color rose swiftly under Angelica's skin and fanned out along the high arch of her cheekbones.

"Put me down!"

Cade's eyes met hers. She could see amusement at her discomfort—and then something different, something that made her feel as if she were standing at the top of a long, spiraling staircase and peering down it into unending darkness.

He gave her a slow, taunting smile. "What's the matter, sugar? Does it upset you to be reminded there are differences between men and women?"

Angelica's color deepened. "No."

He laughed softly. "No, it doesn't bother you? Or no, there are no differences?"

"Mr. Landon, just because you imagine that women can't hold their own in your world—"

"It's not my imagination, sugar, it's a fact," he said pleasantly. His smile grew until it dimpled his cheek. "But that's not exactly the kind of difference I was referring to."

She swallowed dryly. "If you're any sort of gentleman, Mr. Landon, you'll put me down."

Cade's gaze dropped to Angelica's mouth. It looked soft and faintly swollen, almost as if he'd just kissed her. What would she do if he did?

"Cade," he said, his voice slightly thick.

"What?"

His eyes lifted to hers. "My name is Cade," he said.

Angelica swallowed again. "Please put me down— Cade."

He said nothing, and her heart gave a wild beat. What if he refused to let go? What if he lowered his head, brought his lips to hers, kissed her until she was, indeed, tumbling down that long, spiraling staircase?

But he didn't. He simply dropped her the last couple of inches to the floor as if she was an unwanted package, folded his arms over his chest and glared at her.

"You might try saying thank you," he said.

Angelica snatched up her jacket and thrust her arms into it. "Just think," she said coldly, "I might have broken my neck." She tugged down her skirt, smoothed her hair, then shoved her chair to the desk. "Think of how happy that would have made you!"

"You're wrong, Miss Gordon."

"Really?" Her smile was saccharine sweet. "I'm touched."

"A broken neck would have landed you in the hospital, which would have meant increased insurance costs for Landon Enterprises." His smile was as cloyingly sweet as hers. "Assuming you've been paying the premiums, of course."

Angelica flushed. "Certainly, I've been paying the premiums," she said, and made a mental note to check. "Now, what do you want?"

Cade laughed. He picked up the scarred chair that stood opposite the desk, spun it around and straddled it.

"That's easy. I want my company."

Angelica sat down, folded her hands on the desk and gazed at him with bright-eyed interest.

"What company?" she said politely.

My, my, my, Cade thought, the lady was good at this. She'd been flustered as hell a few minutes ago, as out of her league at the mildest sort of male-female banter as a spinster at a bachelor party. But now that they were on more familiar ground, she was back in charge.

At least, she assumed she was. Easy, Cade told himself, just take it slow and easy.

"You know what I'm talking about," he said. "Gordon Oil."

"I thought we'd settled that yesterday."

"Not quite." He waited, giving it all the time he could. "I spoke with my attorney last evening."

Angelica lifted a hand to her hair. A nervous gesture, Cade wondered, or was the habit of trying to subdue that coppery mane such an old one that she was unaware of it? It was useless anyway; their little tussle had brought a halo of ringlets to bounce lightly at her temples.

His eyes narrowed. When he'd come through that door and spotted her balanced on that chair, his brain had told him it had to be Angelica Gordon—who else could it have been? But, in the split second he'd had to get to her before she fell, he'd found himself wondering.

Could Angelica Gordon have legs that went on forever? Could she have such a gently rounded bottom? Could she have breasts that looked as if they might just fill a man's cupped palms?

The message he'd gotten once he'd had her in his arms was a definite yes.

Amazing, he thought, how different she looked sitting behind that desk in an outfit no woman who thought of herself as a woman would wear, looking as if she'd never given that little breathless shudder when she'd felt the hardness of his quickening body against hers.

"What are you thinking, Mr. Landon?"

Cade cleared his throat. "I don't think you want to know, Miss Gordon."

"You're right, if it's another diatribe about how you want me out of this office. You'll be wasting your breath."

He smiled. "My legal people say otherwise, Angelica."

She stiffened. "What did you call me?"

"Angelica. That is your name, isn't it?"

"Yes, but..." But what? Why should the sound of her own name so surprise her?

Maybe it was because it was months since anyone had used it. The men who worked for her had flatly refused.

"We couldn't do that, ma'am," they'd said.

But she couldn't let them call her Miss Gordon. The male-female barrier was artificial and counterproductive. Every book that dealt with the psychology of leadership made that clear.

Eventually, one brave soul had addressed her as A.H. The nickname had stuck. Emily had adopted it and Angelica had even come to think of herself that way. Now, to hear her name on Cade's lips...

Wasn't there some pagan superstition that said you were in jeopardy if the enemy learned your name?

"Well? Is Angelica your name, or isn't it?"

Angelica looked at Cade. Stop being dumb, she told herself sharply, and she nodded.

"It is."

"Good. At least we agree on something."

Cade rose and began walking around the cramped office. He frowned at the stack of mail on Angelica's desk, ran his finger over the computer printouts that hung like torn wallpaper from the printer in the corner, finally paused beside a bank of file cabinets. He peered at the labeled drawers, then pulled one open.

"Where do you keep your current inventory listing?"

Angelica's chair squealed in protest as she shoved it back.

"What do you think you're doing?"

"Is this it?" he said, taking a folder from the drawer.

She snatched it. "I don't know what game you think you're playing—"

"Not me, sugar. I've been on the up and up since I walked in here yesterday."

He reached past her and took out another folder, but Angelica grabbed it from him, too.

"Cade," she said through her teeth, "I have a busy schedule this morning, and—"

"You don't have any kind of schedule this morning."

"That's nonsense! Did Emily tell you that? Because if she did—"

"She didn't have to. I looked at your appointment calendar."

Color flamed in Angelica's face. She turned, slapped the file folders on her desk, then put her hands on her hips.

"You have two minutes to walk out that door," she said coldly. "After that, I'll call the police and tell them you're trespassing." Her smile was quick and chill. "And—before you ask—the phone lines are working today."

Cade wanted to laugh, but the woman looked as if she'd slug him if he did. And then he'd be in real trouble, because he knew he'd retaliate by picking her up, turning her over his knee and giving her the paddling she so roundly deserved.

Besides, Grant had warned him. Be cool, be subtle and find out what you can.

He took a deep breath. "Look, I didn't come here to quarrel. I came for information. You made a statement yesterday, and—"

"And you want proof."

His eyes narrowed. She sounded so composed. *Was* there proof? Had two crazy old men hacked out a memorandum that would give Landon's legal department ulcers for the millennium?

"Yes," he said, his eyes never leaving her face, "I do."

Angelica nodded. She turned, walked around her desk and sat down.

"My father and yours had a verbal agreement."

Cade gave her a tight smile. Landon's legal eagles might still end up with ulcers, but at least he'd been prepared for this.

"Really," he said, his face expressionless. He watched her for a long moment but she didn't stir or even blink. "Why?"

"What do you mean, why?"

"Why would my father have agreed to such a foolish restriction?"

Angelica bit her lip. Why, indeed? It was a good question, an excellent question. Sooner or later, she'd have to come up with an answer. For the time being, all she could do was bluff.

"I've no idea," she said politely. "But then, figuring out your father's motives isn't my problem."

A muscle knotted in Cade's jaw. "You'll have to do better than that."

Angelica permitted herself a small, self-satisfied smile. "I don't have to do anything," she said, leaning back in her chair.

"No?"

"No. If you decide to contest my right to remain in charge of this company—"

"*If* I decide to contest it?"

Cade's voice sounded soft, almost silken; only later would she realize that it was neither, that it was, instead, dark with menace.

"Why, yes," she said, almost pleasantly. "If you should choose to contest my right—"

Cade came around the desk so fast that all she could do was gasp. He bent to her, clasped her by the shoulders and hauled her to her feet.

"This is *my* company, and don't you forget it. As for your story that there was some kind of verbal agreement..." He smiled coldly. "Hell, sugar, that doesn't mean a damn. It's nothing but a bold-faced lie!"

Angelica stared at him, fire blazing in her eyes. "I refuse to dignify that remark with an answer!"

"What's the matter, sugar? Afraid of the truth?"

"Don't call me that!"

"Don't call you what?"

"Sugar," she said with ice in her voice.

His smile was taut and mirthless. "Why not? Does it offend your lamebrain feminist agenda?"

"Listen here, you—you bully—"

"Me? A bully?" Cade laughed, but his eyes were chill. "Hell, I think I've been more than civil, all things considered."

"Goodbye, Cade. We have nothing more to say to each other."

His hands tightened on her, until she could feel the press of each finger.

"You know what I think? I think you'd label any man who stood up to you a bully."

Angelica laughed. "You've got to be kidding! You come strutting into my office as if you were some—some jackbooted storm trooper and order me out as if I were just a poor little female and then you get annoyed when I call you what you are?" She tossed her head. "What's the problem, Cade? Don't you know what to do with a woman like me?"

It was a stupid thing to have said, she knew that as soon as she'd said it, but it was too late. Cade laughed and his arms went around her.

"Hell," he said, "I know *exactly* what to do with a woman like you."

She cried out as his mouth dropped to hers. Her hands came up in defence and fisted against his chest but he only drew her closer.

"Stop it," she said fiercely, twisting her face from his, "stop it, do you hear me? The only thing you're proving is that I'm right, that you are a bully—"

His mouth covered hers again as he spun her around and trapped her against the desk. His hands went into her hair, pulling out the rubber band that held it at her nape, and coppery curls spilled into his waiting fingers.

Cade twisted the strands around his hand and kissed her harder.

Angelica began to tremble. She wanted to push him from her, to hit him and tell him he was everything she despised . . .

Oh, but the feel of his mouth on hers! The feel of that hard, powerful body, the thought of the callused hands on her soft, expectant flesh, the honeyed surrender that would be possible with a man like him . . .

Cade took her face in his hands. "Open your mouth," he said, in a voice thick with passion. "Let me taste you."

Liquid heat shot through her blood. With a soft whimper of mindless submission, she gave him her mouth, parting her lips to the thrust of his tongue, letting him fill her with his taste. Her hands opened; she spread them over his chest, curling her fingers into his shirt, measuring his thundering heartbeat.

Cade drew her jacket from her shoulders, trapping her within its soft folds. He bent his head and pressed his lips to her throat while he whispered her name, and then his hands moved lightly over her sweater and cupped her breasts. Angelica gave a startled cry as she felt his hands on her. Blindly, she moved closer to him, her nipples tightening and budding against his seeking palms, her body aching for the hardness of his arousal...

The door slammed open. "A.H.," Emily said, "I really am sorry to bother you and Mr. Landon, but—"

Time stood still. Angelica caught a glimpse of her secretary's frozen face, and then Cade swung toward the door, blocking Angelica from view.

"Yes?" he said, so calmly she knew, without question, that everything that had just happened had been a deliberate, cold-blooded reminder of exactly who held the power here.

"Uh—uh..." Emily gulped audibly. "It's not important. I, uh, I just wanted to—to tell Miss Gordon that—that I was going to take my lunch hour early today."

"That's fine," Cade said, very coolly. "In the future, please check with me first."

Emily nodded, then slipped out the door. As soon as it closed, Angelica spoke.

"You wasted your time," she said coldly. "Nothing you can do will convince me that you're in charge, not that—that disgusting demonstration of macho power or that remark you just made to Emily."

Cade looked at her. A moment ago, he'd thought he might have found a real woman inside Angelica Gordon. But she was nothing but a cold-blooded, headstrong machine, driven by the need to succeed at any cost. As for Gordon Oil—she would rather ruin it than admit she couldn't run it.

London, and Dumai, would have to wait.

CHAPTER FOUR

THERE was no sign of Cade the next day but Angelica wasn't deceived. Maybe she'd scored some points in a verbal skirmish, but the war was far from over.

By late morning, after she'd taken her dusty copy of *Management Psychology* from the shelves and scanned the chapters, her dream of even a small victory had faded. Going head to head with a man like Cade Landon was just playing his game.

And he had all the aces.

Angelica closed the textbook, leaned her elbows on her desk and propped her head in her hands.

"I knew that," she muttered wearily. "I knew that, but I let myself be drawn into an argument anyway."

Damn! If that was the effect the man had on her—if he could get her so blazing angry that she forgot everything she'd ever learned—she was never going to be able to pull off this stunt.

She knew what had to be done. She had to be on her guard, keep from giving him any more chances to confuse her and push her around. The trick was to stay one step ahead of him, to seem to exercise her own power before he had the opportunity to prove his.

The intercom buzzed. Angelica picked up the phone.

"A.H.?" Emily's voice was hushed. "It's Mr. Landon."

Angelica looked at the copy of *Management Psychology* and touched it gently.

"A.H.? Did you hear me?"

"Yes, Emily," she said with studied calmness. "Of course. Tell Mr. Landon to come in."

"I didn't mean he was here, A.H. I meant that he's on line one."

Angelica nodded and steeled herself for the sound of Cade's voice.

"Put him through, please."

Emily cleared her throat. "He, uh, he doesn't want to talk to you."

"He doesn't?" Angelica straightened in her chair. "What does he want, then?"

"He, uh, he wants me to fax some stuff to him at his hotel."

"Stuff?" Angelica said carefully.

"Yes. Purchase orders, contracts, bills—that sort of thing."

Angelica's mouth thinned. "Well, you can tell Mr. Landon that he can take his requests and shove them..." She paused, swallowed hard and glanced at the psychology textbook sitting on her desk. "...and shove them into his briefcase," she finished lamely.

"Uh-huh."

"And Emily—I'm glad you had the presence of mind to check with me before doing anything."

"Well, I would have, of course—but, actually, it was Mr. Landon who suggested it." Emily gave an embarrassed little laugh. "He said that although he has complete authority, he wanted you informed before I followed through on his order. As a courtesy, you know?"

Angelica took a steadying breath. "Fax him whatever he wants," she said. "Just keep a list of the items you provide him, please, so that I know exactly what—"

"Oh, sure. He already told me to do that, too."

Angelica sprang up from her desk, knocking *Management Psychology* to the floor in the process.

"Thank you," she snarled, and slammed down the phone.

A couple of minutes passed. Angelica sighed. She picked up the book, dusted it off and put it back on her desk. Then she stepped out of her office.

"Sorry, Emily," she said. "I let my temper get the best of me for a couple of minutes."

Emily shrugged. "You've been under a lot of stress, A.H. I understand."

"I hope you do. That man, that Cade Landon..."

The telephone rang. Emily picked it up, listened, then put her hand over the mouthpiece.

"It's the bank," she whispered, and handed the phone to Angelica.

"Mr. Carruthers," Angelica said warily. "How nice to hear from you. If this is about the installment that's due on that note—"

But the call had nothing to do with the overdue payment. The banker explained that there was a Mr. Cade Landon in his office.

"He seems to have the necessary authority to see copies of your bank statements, Miss Gordon. I, um, I thought you might wish to be made aware..."

Angelica put her fingers to the bridge of her nose and pinched lightly.

"Yes, I understand," she said evenly. "Thank you for calling."

By late afternoon, the phone was ringing off the hook. Emily's throat rasped and Angelica's head was pounding. The little office had never been besieged with so many calls before.

Apparently, Cade was putting in appearances everywhere, meeting with Angelica's subcontractors, with her messenger service, with the small and large firms that supplied her with parts for the pumps and paper for the office and every damned thing in between.

Angelica looked at *Management Psychology*, still sitting on her desk but now buried under the seemingly endless list of files Emily had faxed to Cade.

Stay calm, she told herself. Don't lose your cool. Be accommodating and businesslike and wait for the right moment to show him the graphs and pie charts and computer printouts that will surely make him understand why it's going to take time to turn things around here.

At five, Emily announced that she was either coming down with the worst cold of her life or losing her voice completely. She was going to go home, brew a pot of tea and climb into bed.

"A good idea," Angelica said wearily. "I think I'll head straight for bed myself, pull the covers up over my head and sleep till—"

"Just be sure and set the alarm clock first."

Angelica spun toward the door. Cade was standing there watching her, just as he had the first time she'd seen him, except this time his expression was grim.

"I'm off," Emily said, her voice a hoarse squeak. She shot Angelica a quick smile and scurried past Cade, out the door.

"Well," Angelica said, forcing a smile to her lips, "what a surprise, Cade. If I'd known you were coming, I'd have asked Emily to prepare coffee or—"

"I didn't come here for coffee."

Angelica's smile wavered just a little. "No, of course not. But you've had such a busy day, I thought—"

"Tell me something, lady. Is there anybody in Dallas you don't owe money to?"

Angelica swallowed hard. Be calm, she told herself, just be calm.

"I know it must seem that way," she said carefully, "but that's only because you're not familiar with the oil business. If you were aware of its special problems and needs, you—"

"You're up to those gorgeous eyes of yours in debt, sugar. Are *you* aware of *that*?"

Gorgeous eyes? Cade frowned. Why in hell had he said that? Dammit, his brain was probably fried, thanks to the hours he'd just spent staring at column after column of red ink.

Not that the woman had noticed his nonsensical slip of the tongue. She was too busy trying to control her temper. Her creamy skin was turning the same color as her hair, and the breasts she seemed so intent on disguising under yet another boxy suit jacket were rising and falling so quickly that it looked as if she'd just broken the record for the mile.

"I'm carrying some debt, yes. But—"

"But," Cade said, "you've got half a dozen charts and printouts to explain the reasons for it."

Angelica frowned. "Emily didn't tell me you'd asked for copies of my audiovisuals."

"Copies of your. . ." Cade began to laugh. "Damn, but that's good! Your audiovisuals, hm? Oh, I like that. I like that a lot."

Angelica's spine stiffened. The desire to slap the arrogant grin from his handsome face was almost overpowering. She turned on her heel, walked to her desk and began stuffing things into her briefcase.

"I'd appreciate it if you'd get to the point. Why are you here?"

"Suppose I said I've come to give you one last chance to admit the truth, that there never was any verbal agreement between your father and mine? What would you say to that?"

"I'd say you were wasting my time and yours. Now, if that's all you want—"

Cade's hand dropped on her shoulder. Angelica caught her breath in surprise. He was such a big man, yet she'd never even heard his footsteps as he crossed the room. But she could feel him behind her now, feel the faint brush of his hard body against hers, the pressure of his fingers as he turned her toward him.

"You do know how to push a man, sugar," he said softly.

She looked up. His eyes were narrowed, the irises enormous and black within narrow bands of deep blue. A smile so dangerous it made her pulse quicken tilted across his mouth.

Why was it so hard to draw breath into her lungs? Why was she so aware of his hand on her shoulder? Layers of fabric separated his fingertips and her bare skin, but still heat seemed to inundate her blood and penetrate to her bones.

Angelica jerked away. "And you," she said sharply, "are making a big mistake if you think I'm some—some wide-eyed little thing you can browbeat into submission. If you came here for a purpose, please get to it. Otherwise, I'd like you to leave. It's been a long day, and—"

"And it's going to be a longer one tomorrow. I'm going out to see the Gordon operation near Odessa in the morning."

Angelica gritted her teeth. "Why tell me? Surely, you haven't suddenly decided to ask permission?"

"I've a general idea where the site is," Cade said, ignoring the challenge, "but I need directions. A map, if you have one."

"Certainly. Directions. A map." Her smile was brittle. "Anything else?"

"Yes. Be sure you remember to set your alarm clock." A smile tilted across his mouth. "I'll be at your door at six, and I don't like to be kept waiting."

She stared after him as he turned and walked off. At the last second, she called after him.

"What do you mean, you'll be at my door at six?" Her voice rose, bearing just a touch of shrillness. "I'm not going with you to Odessa, Cade."

He paused, his hand on the doorknob, and looked at her. "Of course you are," he said gently.

"Don't be ridiculous!" She folded her arms and lifted her chin. "You've spent the day prying into every corner of my life—"

"Of this company's life, sugar. There's a difference."

"The point I'm making," she said coldly, "is that you've managed quite nicely without any help from me. Why you should change your mind now is—"

"Six o'clock. And please dress appropriately." His eyes raked over her, then came to rest on her face. "Those gunnysacks may be the latest thing at Miss Palmer's but they won't stand up to a day out on the West Texas flats."

Angelica flushed. "Just give me one good reason I should go to Odessa with you," she demanded.

The easy laughter fled Cade's face.

"Because I say you will," he snapped, "and because my word is law around here. Is that a good enough reason for you, Angelica?"

The door slammed shut after him. Angelica stood still for a long moment. Then she mouthed a word she'd never before even thought, reached for *Management Psychology* and hurled it into the wastebasket.

Odessa was almost four hundred miles away.

How would she and Cade Landon manage the endless drive without killing each other?

At a quarter to six the next morning, Angelica stepped out on the gently sagging porch of the house that had been her father's. She peered up and down the quiet street and then, with a little sigh, she sat down in an old wicker rocker, folded her hands in her lap and settled in to wait.

She'd debated with herself for the past quarter hour, trying to decide if it was best to be ready when Cade arrived or if it would give her the advantage to keep him cooling his heels. The desire to do just that had been almost overwhelming, but finally common sense had overridden ego.

Making Cade wait would only get him angry, and the day was going to be miserable enough without that kind of start.

She rose, walked to the railing and peered up and down the street. Sunrise had brought a flush of pink to the distant hills and gilded the aspens that stood like sentinels along the curb.

Across the way, an elderly gentleman stood on his porch, drinking coffee and gazing at the first autumn leaves that waited for the touch of the rake. A few houses down, a woman emerged in a green jogging suit yawned, stretched, then set off at an easy trot.

There was still no sign of Cade.

Frowning, Angelica glanced at her watch. It was almost six. Maybe she should have waited inside. Maybe he was the one who was going to keep her waiting. Maybe—

"Well, you're prompt. That's one thing in your favor, I guess."

She looked up. Cade was standing at the foot of the porch steps, a shiny black pickup truck parked behind him at the curb. Her gaze flew over him. The custommade suits, the white shirts and silk ties, were gone. Even the highly polished boots had been replaced.

He was dressed, instead, in jeans that fit his long legs and narrow hips snugly, and a faded wool shirt with the sleeves rolled back to the elbows. Scuffed, scarred boots showed from beneath his jeans and a cap bearing the logo of the Colorado Rockies baseball team was pulled down low over his forehead.

This, Angelica thought, bristling, was no way to pay a visit to a company installation. Cade didn't look professional, he didn't look managerial, he didn't look like he was the man in charge. He looked like one of the roughnecks who worked the rigs, he looked—he looked...

Her mouth went dry. He looked more handsome than any man had a right to look.

She frowned. Who cared how he looked? Cade Landon could look like a stand-in for Bela Lugosi, for all it mattered to her.

"Dammit, Angelica, what in hell are you wearing?"

Cade was glaring at her angrily. She leaned away from the rail, looked down at her seersucker suit, then at him.

"What do you mean, what am I wearing?"

"Don't answer a question with a question, woman. What do you call that outfit you've got on?"

"It's a suit," she said coolly. "I'm sure you've heard the word before."

Cade tilted his cap back. His eyes were very blue in the early morning light.

"I told you we were going to Odessa," he said. "But you're dressed for the office."

"I am dressed for a day in the field."

He gave her a pitying smile. "According to who? The guy who wrote *Dress for Success*?"

"Make fun all you like, Cade, but if you knew anything about managing people—"

"I hate to disappoint you, sugar, but I manage people all the time."

"Oh, yes," she said with a disdainful smile. "And I'll bet they jump through hoops. After all, you're the great Cade Landon, of Landon Enterprises."

"Jesus, here it comes." Cade rolled his eyes to the heavens. "The lecture about how tough it is to claw and fight your way to the top."

"No lectures," Angelica said coldly, "just a common sense piece of advice. Don't try to pretend you're one of the boys. It doesn't work, and the men won't respect you for it."

"A brilliant analysis, I'm sure. Now, go on into that house and change into a pair of jeans."

"Listen, Cade, you may have the right to tell me what to do at the office, but when it comes to my personal life, to what I wear, for goodness sake, *I* make my own decisions! Is that clear?"

Cade shook his head in disgust. The woman was incredible. The time he'd spent poking into her business affairs had convinced him she probably shouldn't even be trusted to keep her own checkbook, she had the disposition of a desert viper, and now it turned out she just about had the common sense of one, too.

He'd made it clear where they were going to spend the day. They were going to inspect half a dozen oil wells in the middle of nowhere, and here she was, dressed for that damned fool girl's school—which was exactly where she belonged. He took a breath, then let it go. Hell, there was no sense in dwelling on that until he had a surefire way to get rid of her.

Until then, he was just going to have to put up with her—but on his terms. And, right at this minute, that meant he'd be damned if he'd take a woman with her legs hanging out—well, considering the length of her skirts, it was her ankles that were hanging out, but the principle was the same.

He absolutely was not going to let a woman dressed the way she was stroll around a place where there were snakes, scorpions and enough mean equipment to ruin anybody's day.

And that hair, he thought furiously. Why did she insist on pulling it back like that? Why didn't she let it hang loose, soft and silky down her back—

"What are you looking at?"

Cade blinked. What in God's name did her hair have to do with anything?

"At a woman who hasn't got the sense she was born with," he snarled. "A seersucker suit and shoes like that for a day in the oil fields—unbelievable!"

"What's the matter?" Angelica asked, with a too-sweet smile. "Are you afraid the crew will take me for the boss and you for just another dime-store cowboy?"

He was up the steps and next to her before she could finish the sentence. He caught hold of her wrist, putting just enough pressure on it so she knew it would be a mistake to try to twist free.

"You've got sharp claws, sugar," he whispered, "and an even sharper mouth." He moved closer, his eyes dark and unreadable in the shadow cast by the bill of his cap. His hands moved to her face and clasped it, and all at once his voice thickened. "Maybe somebody ought to soften that mouth just a little."

Slowly, slowly, his head dipped toward hers. She took a steadying breath, gearing herself for the harsh stamp of male authority she knew had to be coming...

But when his mouth touched hers, it was in the softest of kisses. His lips moved over hers in a clinging caress.

Angelica made a soft sound that might have been protest or acceptance. Her head tilted back like a flower on a stem, her eyes closed—and with a swiftness that left her swaying, Cade let her go.

"If you own anything as common as a pair of jeans," he said in an expressionless voice, "go put them on. Trousers, otherwise. And boots, if you have them, or at least a pair of sturdy shoes."

He saw the defiance flash in her eyes, but that was better than the blur of confusion that had been there seconds ago.

Kissing her had been crazy. Hell, there were better ways to silence a woman like this.

And yet, as she went on standing there, meeting his gaze without backing down, Cade felt the blood begin to thrum in his ears.

What if she really did defy him? He wouldn't—he couldn't—let her get away with it.

Was he going to have to pick her up bodily and carry her into that little house, up the stairs to whatever dark bedroom was hers? Her mouth, even that vicious tongue, would soften then, he was sure of it. Every part of her would turn soft under his lips and his hands, until finally she would cry out his name and beg him to bury himself inside her...

The unbidden images sent a sharp wave of desire coursing through his body, tightening every muscle he possessed. Something of what he was feeling must have shown in his face because Angelica suddenly took a step back.

"You're a despicable human being," she hissed, and she turned and fled.

Cade stood still for a moment. Then he gave a shaky laugh, turned and trotted down the steps. He wasn't despicable. He was stupid. When you started having fantasies about women like Angelica Gordon, you were in trouble. What man knew that better than he?

Too much Texas sun, he thought, and he climbed into the rented truck, tilted back the seat, pulled down his cap and settled in to wait.

He had the definite feeling Angelica was going to take her own sweet time about reappearing.

After five minutes on the road, it was obvious Cade wasn't heading for Interstate 20, the highway that tied Dallas and Fort Worth to West Texas. He steered the pickup down one narrow dirt road after another, always, Angelica noticed with displeasure, driving at least ten miles over the speed limit.

"This isn't the way to Odessa," she finally said, when they had to stop at a train crossing. Cade didn't answer, and her voice rose a little. "I said, this is not the way to my wells."

"No," he said with a tight smile. "It's the way to mine."

Angelica's eyes flashed. "Very witty, but—"

"Did you bring the map I asked for?"

"Yes, but what's the point if—"

The crossing gates lifted. Cade shifted into gear and the truck shot forward.

"Plot us the most direct way to get from Route 302, just outside Notrees, to the wells."

"Notrees? But why would we—"

"Can you figure a route, Angelica? Or would you rather I did it myself?"

She glared at him, then whipped the map from her purse and snapped it open.

"Notrees to the wells," she said, "yes, sir, Mr. Landon, sir."

Cade laughed. "Now you're getting the idea, sugar."

She shot him another furious look, then buried her face in the map. When she looked up again, they were on a dusty airfield, pulling alongside a small aircraft.

"What is this?" she said in surprise.

"A Piper Apache," Cade answered, deadpan.

"You know what I mean, dammit! Did you rent a plane? The company can't afford—"

"Gordon can't." He opened his door and got out of the truck. "But I can. Well? Are you coming, or are you just going to sit there?"

Angelica muttered something, threw open her door and stepped down to the ground. She walked toward Cade, who was already standing in the open doorway of the small plane. He held out his hand, but she ignored it and hoisted herself inelegantly on board.

"It must be nice to own a company that has money to burn," she said coldly.

Cade didn't bother answering. The money he was burning today was strictly his own, but that was none of her business.

"Where's the pilot?"

"You're looking at him," he said with a lazy smile.

"You mean—" Angelica stared at him as he climbed into the pilot's seat. "You mean, you're driving this thing?"

"I'm flying it, yes." He reached out, tapped a gauge on the instrument panel, then looked at her and grinned. "You're as transparent as glass, sugar. What's the matter? Do you want to see my license before you trust yourself to my tender, loving care?"

Angelica tossed her head. "I'd sooner trust a scorpion," she said, and flounced into the seat beside him, "but what choice do I have?"

Cade laughed. "None at all," he said, and Angelica gritted her teeth at how very true that was.

* * *

The flight was smooth, she had to admit, and Cade seemed to be a competent pilot. And it was fascinating to watch the West Texas landscape unroll beneath them, juniper and oak-covered hills giving way to the mesquite and scrub oak of the plains.

Still, Angelica was relieved when the Apache began its descent. There was something disconcerting about sitting close beside Cade in the little plane, the warm sunlight heating the cabin. It was too intimate, too much like—like being the last people on the planet.

He brought the Apache to a stop in a place that seemed devoid of life and climbed down from the plane. Angelica ignored his outstretched hand, as she had at the start of the flight, and jumped to the ground herself.

The wind moaned and whipped at her hair. Except for a fast-moving horned lizard, a lonely stand of pump jacks and a dusty pickup truck that might have been the twin to the one they'd left behind in Dallas, they were alone.

"So much for your navigation skill," Angelica said with a frosty smile. "I hate to tell you this, but we're nowhere near—"

Cade went to the truck, opened the door and got behind the wheel. An instant later the engine coughed to life. He rolled down the window and looked at Angelica.

"Well? Are you coming?"

Damn, she thought, and started toward him. The wind snatched at her hair again and the coated rubber band that had secured it flew off. The copper-colored strands burst free and slapped across her face.

With grim determination, she climbed into the truck and slammed the door.

Cade stepped on the gas, and the truck lurched over the rutted road. Questions danced through Angelica's mind. Where had Cade gotten this truck? Whose was it? How had he made arrangements to have it here, ready and waiting?

"I have a buddy lives in Notrees." Angelica swung toward him. His eyes were on the road ahead. "I called him last night, asked him if he had something he could leave out here for me to use."

"Fascinating," Angelica said politely.

Cade sighed. "What route do I take?"

The one straight to hell, she wanted to say. But she didn't. Cade was about to have a very bad day. He'd had a free hand so far, but if he really imagined his pseudo-work outfit and his pickup truck were going to win him any points from a gang of roughnecks, he was in for a big surprise. Men who sweated to wrest oil from the earth hadn't won their nickname for their charm.

"Well?" Cade said dryly. "Do you want to tell me how to get to the Gordon site or shall I guess?"

"Take the first right after we get on the main road and I'll direct you from there."

"Fine."

Better than fine, Angelica thought.

Cade Landon, captain of industry, was about to meet his Waterloo—and she was going to relish every moment.

A couple of hours later, Angelica was sitting on a wooden bench in the dubious shade of a scrub oak, trying to hang onto a smile that felt as if it had been pasted on her face.

Lunch had just ended, and a good thing, too. It had been an impromptu feast, with Cade—and with her, the men kept insisting, though anyone could see it was an out-and-out lie—as guests of honor.

Two hours, she thought glumly, two whole hours of Cade and the crew exchanging hair-raising tales of derring-do in the Middle East, in Texas, in Oklahoma and in places she'd never heard of before, accompanied by enough oversize sandwiches and long-necked bottles of beer to keep a small army happy.

Now, her men—*her* men, dammit—had whisked Cade off to show him some piece of equipment that had them all close to ecstasy, leaving her behind.

"You just sit here and stay comfortable," Tom, her foreman, had crooned.

Angelica's jaw tightened. "Damn you to hell, Cade Landon," she muttered under her breath. "You're nothing but a lying, sneaking rat!"

She had spent the past couple of days gloating over how he didn't know a thing about the oil business only to learn that, as far as her crew was concerned, Cade Landon *was* the oil business!

At first, things had gone as she'd expected. Her foreman had greeted her with polite resignation when she'd stepped down from the pickup truck.

"Miss Angelica," he'd said, "I mean, A.H. What a nice surprise. We had no idea you were comin' to visit."

Angelica had smiled as she offered her hand. "I brought someone with me, Tom," she'd said. "He represents Landon Enterprises and he'd like to take a look around."

It had been hard not to laugh at the look that had come over Tom's weathered face.

"That's just what we need, on top of everything else," he'd muttered. "A guy who don't know oil wells from inkwells, come to tell us how many drill bits we should use and how many feet of pipe—"

"Hey, man, you've got it all wrong." Cade's voice had been as cheerful as his smile as he'd stepped past Angelica, his hand outthrust. "You guys are the experts here. You're gonna have to explain things to me."

Angelica ground her teeth in frustration as she remembered the look—part shock, part quizzical recognition—that had come over her foreman's face.

"Don't I know you?" he'd said, and Cade had grinned modestly, all but scuffed his toes in the dust and said, well, maybe, considering that he'd spent his life—his *life,* damn him!—in the oil business, yeah, maybe Tom just might have seen him around.

"I'm Cade Landon," he'd said, and Tom had gone white.

"*Cade* Landon? That's the Landon Miss Angelica—I mean, A.H.—brought us?"

"Yeah," Cade had said, while Tom pumped his hand. "Nice to meet you."

"Cade Landon," Tom had repeated, still stunned. "For crissakes, A.H., why didn't you tell us... Oh. Hey, sorry. I didn't mean to cuss, Miss Angelica, I—shit! I mean—"

Cade had slapped the man lightly on the back. "The lady understands, Tom. In fact, she wants you to forget about calling her by her initials. Isn't that right, Angelica?"

By then, Angelica had been incapable of saying anything. Not that it had mattered. Tom was too busy. He'd called the other men over and soon the whole bunch had been clustered around Cade as if he were either the patron saint of oil exploration or the latest incarnation of Elvis Presley, and from that point on it had been all downhill.

A hard male arm came looping around Angelica's shoulders. She stiffened, looked up into Cade's smiling face and whispered a word that made his eyebrows lift toward his hairline.

"Why, sugar," he said softly, "I'm shocked! I never dreamed they let you talk that way at Miss Palmer's."

"You—you liar," she said. "You cheat! You no-good, miserable son of a—"

"Miss Angelica?"

Angelica looked around, glowering. Her foreman was standing at the center of a little group of roughnecks, beaming at her.

"Yes?" she snapped. "What is it?"

"We just want you to know—the boys and me, that is—look, maybe we ain't always done things the way you'd have liked. It wasn't nothing personal, Miss

Angelica, it was—the thing is, you don't know this business." He shuffled uneasily from one foot to the other, looked to Cade for a nod of approval and cleared his throat. "If only you'd said it was Cade, here, who'd be okaying your orders—"

"She's speechless," Cade said quickly, as Angelica drew in her breath. "Isn't that right?" His eyes flashed a warning as he drew Angelica to her feet. "Just give us some room, boys. I want to walk Miss Angelica around, explain some of what we discussed."

When they'd put some distance between themselves and the crew, Angelica jabbed her elbow into Cade's ribs.

"Let go of me," she snarled.

"Only if you promise to behave."

"Why should I? You're a lying, cheating, no-good—"

Cade laughed softly. "What's that old saying about the pot calling the kettle black?"

Angelica flushed. "I've no idea what you're talking about."

"I'll just bet you don't. Anyway, you wouldn't want to upset the guys, would you?"

She swung to face him, bracing her hand on a pump jack for leverage.

"The *guys*," she said through her teeth, "can go to hell."

"You don't mean that. They're a damned good bunch. I even know a couple of them, had them working for me in the Gobi—"

"Why didn't you tell me you were an oilman?"

He smiled. "You didn't ask."

"Ask? What do you mean, I didn't ask? I didn't have to ask, dammit. You should have said—"

"Why would I have said anything?" Cade was still smiling, but his eyes had turned cold. "You'd already made up your mind that you knew everything there was to know about me, that I was a hatchet man, a human calculator—''

"Isn't it bad enough you came down here to steal Gordon's from me? You didn't have to make a fool of me, too.''

"Are we back to that? If there's a thief here, sugar, it's you. This company is no more yours than it is the man in the moon's.''

"And that's another thing! I hate, abhor and despise being called sugar.''

"It's a hell of an improvement over going through life being known as A.H.''

"There's nothing wrong with being called by one's initials!''

"No, not if you're fat, fifty and you've got five o'clock shadow!''

"Go on, laugh all you like. But for your information, it was the men right here who dubbed me A.H.''

"Come on, lady! No self-respecting roughneck would ever want to address a woman as anything but miss! If they finally settled on calling you by a pair of initials, they must have been desperate!''

Angelica flushed. "It was a most satisfactory compromise,'' she said stiffly, "one that overcame the formality so out of place in today's workplace without putting the men in a position that made them feel uncomfortable.''

Cade shook his head in disbelief. "Is that a direct quote, or did you make it up for my benefit?''

"Don't speak to me as if I were stupid!''

"Look, maybe what you learned in those books of yours might work in some uptight corporate world. But this business is different. Oil crews pride themselves on their masculinity—it's why they're called roughnecks.''

"And don't patronize me, either!''

"I'm only trying to make you see reason. Dammit, Angelica, what if it turned out you were telling me the truth, that there was some kind of verbal agreement putting you in charge of Gordon's—''

He stopped, but it was too late. Angelica was already smiling.

"What did you say?''

"Don't take that as any kind of acknowledgment,'' he growled. "It was just a supposition. It didn't mean a thing.''

"Of course it meant something. You just admitted that—''

"Jesus.'' Cade's face went white. "Angelica,'' he said, "shut up!''

"Shut up?'' She laughed. "Listen, Cade, just because these men treated you like some little tin god doesn't mean—''

"Dammit, I'm not joking! Stand absolutely still.''

Her laughter faded. There was something about the look on Cade's face...

Something whispered across her fingers. Her heart leaped into her throat. "Cade?'' she said, her eyes locked on his.

"Don't move,'' he said grimly. "Not an inch. I'm going to—''

A sharp pain stabbed into the tender flesh just below her thumb. Cade cursed, leaped forward and batted a dark, evil-looking creature to the ground.

"A scorpion,'' Angelica whispered, shuddering as Cade ground the thing under his heel.

"Angelica,'' Cade said, pulling her into his arms. "Did it sting you? Let me see your hand.''

She looked at the dead scorpion and then at Cade, her face as white as chalk.

"Remember when I said it would be better to trust a scorpion than to trust you?'' she whispered. "I was wrong. It turns out you can't trust a scorpion, either.''

She tried to smile, but it didn't work. Instead, her eyes rolled upward and she collapsed in Cade's arms.

CHAPTER FIVE

LIGHT. Bright, white light, a blinding circle of it, beaming down from above, and beneath Angelica there stretched a hard, cold surface. There was an acrid, chemical tang in the air...and skittering toward her was something evil and ugly, something that carried its barbed tail upraised.

Angelica began to struggle. She had to get away before the creature reached her.

Hands clasped her shoulders, held her fast as she tried to run.

"Easy, sugar," a voice whispered.

"No," she said desperately, "no! The scorpion..."

"Open your eyes," the voice demanded. "You can do it. Come on, sugar. Open your eyes and look at me."

She didn't want to; she wanted to fall back into the darkness. But denying the soft, firm voice was impossible.

Her lashes fluttered.

"That's it, sugar. Just a little more."

Slowly, Angelica's lashes lifted from her cheeks, and she found herself looking into eyes so darkly blue they seemed like bottomless bits of sky.

"Cade?" she whispered.

"Yes," Cade said. His gaze swept across her face. "How do you feel?"

Angelica moistened her lips as she considered the question. Her head pounded, her right arm ached, her hand felt as if someone had numbed it and then hung a fifty-pound weight from her fingertips.

"Like I've been run over by a truck," she said finally. "Everything hurts."

"Do you remember what happened?"

She nodded. "I—there was a scorpion, and..."

A shudder racked her body. Cade cursed softly, put his arms around her and drew her close.

"The damned thing stung you, and it was all my fault. I didn't get it in time. I was afraid it would get you if I moved too fast, but—"

"I should have been more careful," Angelica whispered. "Everybody knows you have to look out for scorpions in this part of Texas."

"Yeah, but scorpions aren't supposed to climb pump jacks."

Angelica drew back a little and looked at Cade. "Then, it was the scorpion's fault," she said, smiling slightly. "He was in a place he had no right to be."

Cade laughed softly. "Now, why didn't I think of that?" he said, and gathered her into his arms again. She closed her eyes, letting herself take comfort in the steady beat of the heart beneath her ear, in the warmth of the arms that held her, in the clean, male scent that filled her nostrils, and then she drew back.

"My—my hand?" she asked, her eyes on Cade's.

He smiled. "The wound was nasty, but there won't be any permanent damage."

Angelica breathed a sigh of relief. "Thank goodness. I've never been sure what a scorpion can really do to you. I mean, I've heard stories, but—"

"I know. I've seen quite a few stings and they've ranged from nothing worse than a bee sting to big-time trouble." He reached out and stroked a tangle of damp copper curls from her forehead. "Thanks to Tom, we got you to the hospital in record time."

Angelica looked around her, at the white-tiled walls, the curtain-draped doorway, the glass-fronted cabinet filled with shiny instruments. Needles, she thought, needles jabbing her...

She shuddered again.

"What is it?" Cade demanded. "Do you feel ill?"

"No, no, it's not that." A quick, embarrassed smile flashed across her face. "I'm a terrible coward about needles, and that case over there is full of them."

He chuckled. "It's probably just as well you were out cold, sugar. You've been poked and prodded and jabbed I don't know how many times with everything from adrenaline to tetanus antitoxin to an antibiotic to some kind of painkiller—" He smiled. "The important thing is that you're going to be fine."

Angelica sighed and closed her eyes. "I can't believe how exhausted I feel," she murmured. "As if I'd been awake for days and days."

"Stress," Cade said softly, "that's all it is, sugar. You need some sleep."

"Mm," she said, and sighed again.

Cade held her gently, one hand massaging her back, the other stroking her hair. He shut his eyes, inhaling the scent of it. Roses, he thought, she smelled of roses, even after all the dust and the sweat and the stink of this place.

His arms tightened around her and he turned his face just enough so his mouth was pressed against her temple. God, she felt so soft. So feminine.

So fragile.

He had to get her out of here. She was worn out; he could feel it in the way she lay in his arms. She needed to lie in a soft bed, not on this cold table. She needed to lie back against clean white sheets, to lie in his arms, to—

"Miss Gordon?"

Cade sprang back, although his hands still clasped Angelica's shoulders. He turned to the doorway where a woman in a white trouser suit stood framed before the curtains, a questioning smile on her face.

"Yes," Angelica said, "that's—"

"Miss Gordon is resting," Cade said. "May I help you?"

The woman ignored him. "How are you feeling, Miss Gordon?"

"OK, I guess."

"She's exhausted," Cade said, frowning.

The woman nodded. "I see." She looked at Cade's hands, still clasping Angelica's shoulders, then at him. "If you wouldn't mind. .?" He hesitated, then stepped back, and she took Angelica's uninjured wrist between her fingers.

"What are you doing?" Cade said.

"I'm taking Miss Gordon's pulse."

"Obviously. But why? She's already been examined." He smiled tightly. "By a physician."

The woman laughed. "Oh, I know that. But I'm here to examine her again."

Angelica cleared her throat. "Cade, maybe you should wait outside. I mean—"

"For what reason? Miss Gordon has been through a lot the past couple of hours. I see no need to subject her to any more questions."

The woman sighed. "I take it you're Mr. Landon?"

Cade nodded. "Yes, that's right."

"The gentleman who rode roughshod over our admittance procedures."

Cade's eyes narrowed. "Indeed," he said dryly.

"The admitting clerk was only doing her job, Mr. Landon. She has to ask questions."

"And I'll be glad to answer them," he said, "but not when I've got a sick woman in my arms."

"Cade?" Angelica said in a puzzled tone. "What's she talking about? Was there a problem?"

"No problem at all," he said, folding his arms over his chest. "I just took exception to being stopped at the door by a sycophant with a clipboard full of forms to sign when what you needed was medical attention."

"Well, thank you for that, but if there are forms that I need to fill out—"

"I'm not here to ask you to fill out forms, Miss Gordon," the woman said. "I simply want to run some quick tests."

"Why?" Cade's voice was sharp. "Is there reason to think something's been overlooked?"

"No, Mr. Landon, not at all. It's simply standard procedure."

"Cade," Angelica said quickly, "really, I appreciate your concern but I can speak for myself."

"You see, Mr. Landon? Miss Gordon understands that I've no wish to bother her."

"But you are bothering her. Can't you see she's in pain?"

Angelica gave a weak laugh. "Listen, you two," she said, "if somebody would just take the time to ask my opinion—"

"Where is the doctor who examined Miss Gordon?" Cade said coldly. "If she needs to have her vital signs checked, I want a physician to do it."

"Hey." Angelica rose on one elbow. "Did you hear what I said? Haven't you forgotten—"

"I *am* a physician, Mr. Landon. I'm Dr. Broderick, chief of toxicology."

"Oh." Cade's cheeks reddened but his grim look didn't change. "Well, why didn't you say so in the first place?"

"For God's sake!" Angelica's voice rang out sharply in the small room. Cade swung toward her and she shot him a look filled with indignation. "What is the matter with you? My hand was injured, not my head. I'm perfectly capable of speaking for myself."

Cade opened his mouth, then shut it. Of course, Angelica Gordon could speak for herself. She could more than speak for herself. She'd proved that to him half a dozen times already.

He looked from Angelica to the doctor. Jesus, he thought, and gave an inward groan. He was making an absolute ass of himself!

He smiled. At least, he tried to.

"Of course," he said, very calmly, as if nothing unusual had happened. "I'll, ah, I'll just step outside and see about those forms."

Damn, damn, damn! he thought as he marched out the door, what a performance.

All right. So he hated the red tape of bureaucracy. So he despised rules that were imposed for the sake of conformity, scorned people who got their kicks out of enforcing those rules. He knew all that about himself, had known those things for years.

But he was a little old to still be battling the demons of his childhood. He drew a deep breath, then let it out through his teeth. And, if he forced himself to be honest, what he felt about unnecessary rules had little to do with what had just happened, with what had been happening since he'd come storming through the doors of the hospital with Angelica in his arms.

It wasn't officious clerks he was fighting, it was terror—the terror he'd felt when Angelica had collapsed out on the oil field. Holding her still body, he'd been struck by how frighteningly defenseless she'd seemed, like a beautiful rose suddenly stripped of its thorns.

He looked down the corridor to where the admitting clerk sat. He still wasn't in the mood to deal with forms and stupid questions, not with a toxicologist in that room with Angelica. Was it really standard procedure, or had they come up with something they hadn't thought of before?

The desire to rip apart the curtain and demand answers was close to overwhelming. Cade cursed under his breath, turned away and paced up the corridor.

Scorpion stings were not uncommon in his world, just as he'd told Angelica. The fiendish creatures tended to inhabit some of the places oil liked best—hot, dry scrubland—and they had the terrible habit of striking first and asking questions later, with the results ranging from vaguely annoying to life-threatening.

The first doctor had said Angelica's wound fell somewhere in between, that it would make her hand and arm swell and would cause her pain but that it would not—that it would not...

"Damn!" Cade's scowl darkened as he swung toward the examination cubicle again.

Not even the ride across the flats had seemed to take this long. He'd never felt so useless in his life, the woman in his arms moaning softly, her hand swelling dangerously despite his immediate attempt to suck out the scorpion's poison, and all he'd been able to do was whisper to her, over and over, that she'd be fine—even though it was a promise that he'd known wasn't really his to make.

Cade's jaw tightened. He should never have taken her out to that damned oil field with him. She didn't belong in the middle of a place like that, no matter what she claimed—but what choice had there been? The woman insisted on claiming that she was in charge of Gordon Oil. Until he could do something about that, she'd be mucking around places where accidents could, and did, happen with terrifying frequency.

Hell, it was just a miracle she hadn't gotten herself injured or worse long before this—

"Mr. Landon?"

Cade swung around, his face dark. Dr. Broderick had drawn open the curtains. Scowling, he started toward her.

"Mr. Landon, I'm delighted to tell you that I agree with my colleague's prognosis. Miss Gordon will recover—uneventfully, I'm certain, and—"

"I assume, Doctor, you explained to Miss Gordon that it would be unfortunate if she got stung again anytime in the near future?"

"Well, no. I didn't."

"Perhaps you should."

Cade looked at Angelica, sitting up on the examining table. She was still pale, her skin drained of all its color by the accident. He wanted to go to her and shake her until her teeth rattled for her foolishness, take her in his arms and kiss her until color flowed back into her ivory skin.

Something knotted in his gut and turned all his worry and confusion to barely contained anger.

"I'm not sure Miss Gordon understands the full implications of what she's done to herself," he said in clipped tones.

"What I did to myself?" Angelica stared at him. "What do you mean, what I did to—"

"Have you explained that the scorpion's venom may have sensitized her, Doctor? That if she's stung again she might well have an allergic reaction?"

"Excuse me," Angelica said. "But—"

"She needs to have some sense put into her head. I haven't managed it, Doctor. Maybe you will."

Angelica stared at him in disbelief. Who had put this man in charge of her life? She'd been stung by a scorpion, not deprived of reason.

"Cade, I'm not a child! I don't need a lecture."

His eyes narrowed. "Whether you do or don't is debatable."

"Mr. Landon," the doctor said, "Mr. Landon, if you'd please calm down—I know you're upset, but—"

"Certainly, I'm upset," he snapped.

Angelica glared at him. "I don't need you to be upset on my account."

"Who the hell said I was? I'm upset because you're my employee. Any time you lose from work will be to my disadvantage."

Silence greeted his outburst. Cade looked at the doctor, whose face told him just what she thought of him, and then at Angelica, who simmered with rage.

Dear God, what an incredibly stupid thing to have said! The worst of it was that he hadn't meant it. Whether Angelica lost time from work was the last thing on his mind.

"Dr. Broderick," Angelica said coldly, "will it be all right if I leave now?"

The doctor offered a grateful smile, one that said she was more than eager to see her do just that.

"Of course, Miss Gordon. I'll just get those tablets for you. One every four hours, remember."

"Yes."

"And take things easy for the next few days."

"I understand."

"Is there someone at home to help you?"

Angelica's chin lifted. "I don't need help, thank you very much. I am perfectly capable of taking care of myself."

"Miss Gordon, when that shot my colleague gave you wears off, your hand and arm are going to hurt like—forgive me, Miss Gordon, but they're going to hurt like hell!"

"You said the tablets would help."

"They will, but they'll also make you groggy. And then there's the problem of dressing yourself, and bathing, and—"

"Thank you for your concern, Doctor, but I'll be fine. Now, if you'd be so good as to arrange for my discharge—oh, and if someone could phone for a taxi, I'd be—"

"Oh, for God's sake!" Cade marched across the room and glared at Angelica. "What is this nonsense? I brought you here and I'll take you back."

Her mouth was a thin, tight line. "I want no help from you, Mr. Landon."

"I'm not giving you a choice, Miss Gordon." He swung toward the doctor. "Did you say something about getting tablets?" The doctor nodded. "Then do so, please."

Angelica's eyes narrowed as the physician hurried off. "Remarkable," she said, "how efficiently you intimidate women, Mr. Landon."

Cade smiled tightly. "Years of practice, Miss Gordon."

"I'm sure of that." She sat up straighter. "But it's not going to work with me. I am leaving here in a taxi, and there's nothing you can do to stop me."

He smiled again, a quick showing of white, predatory teeth.

"We disagree," he said.

"On many things," Angelica said coolly, "especially about my right to speak for myself."

Cade threw up his hands. "Next you'll be quoting passages from the Bill of Rights!"

"Precisely, Mr. Landon. This may be Texas, where men are men and women are not much more than chattel, but the law still applies. In other words," Angelica said, swinging her legs to the floor, "I am a free pers— Oh," she whispered, and reached for the edge of the examining table.

Cade caught her just as her knees buckled.

"You little fool," he growled as he swung her into his arms. "Did you really think you were going to go marching out of here as if nothing had happened to you?"

"Put me down," Angelica said, in a voice that seemed strangely not her own.

"Stop giving orders and start taking them," Cade snarled. "Put your arm around my neck."

She did, because there really was no other choice. He was already leaving the examination cubicle and heading down the corridor. A nurse appeared ahead of them, her eyes rounding at the sight.

"I have some medicine here," she said, "for Miss Angelica Gordon..."

Cade snatched the vial from her hand. "Thank you." When he reached the admitting desk, he paused and looked at the clerk. "I believe you had some questions for Miss Gordon."

The clerk swallowed hard. "I—yes. Yes, sir, I did. About her medical insurance?"

Cade smiled coldly. "Miss Gordon works for the Gordon Oil Company, in Dallas. The company's supposed to have coverage but I'm fairly certain you'll find she's permitted its policy to lapse." He glanced at Angelica. "Isn't that right?"

"Go to hell," she whispered.

"Miss Gordon confirms my supposition," Cade said. "My name is Cade Landon. Send whatever bills she's run up to me care of Gordon Oil. Do you understand?"

"Yes, sir."

Cade nodded. "Fine," he said, and continued toward the front doors.

"I'll pay you back," Angelica said stiffly.

He laughed. "How? Fifty cents a week, for the next hundred years?"

"You addle-brained ape," she said, "you are the most arrogant human being! Put me down this instant, Cade Landon! Do you hear? Put me down!"

"Don't tempt me," he snapped as he shouldered the doors open and made his way down the stairs to the street. "If I put you down, you'd fall on your nose and they'd carry you right back inside and put you to bed." He gave her a chill smile as he strode toward the pickup truck parked at the curb. "Have you ever spent any time in a hospital, Angelica?"

"No. And I'm not in the habit of getting in the way of scorpions, either."

"No," Cade said coldly, "no, you're just a woman who passes out at the sight of a sharp needle—which is what hospitals are full of. The vampires in white coats keep coming around to siphon out blood." He smiled tightly. "Think what fun you'd have."

"You're a bastard, Cade Landon," Angelica said weakly. "An absolute, gold-plated bastard!"

Ahead of them, Tom shot from the driver's seat, hurried around the side of the truck and yanked open the passenger door.

"How is she?" he said worriedly, as Cade climbed inside and settled Angelica in his lap.

"She's still sharp-tongued as a snake, mean-tempered as a mule and headstrong as a goat."

The foreman smiled with relief as he put the truck in gear.

"She's gonna be OK, you mean?"

Cade felt the tension flowing out of him as the hospital fell farther and farther behind.

"Yeah," he said, "she's going to be fine."

Angelica lifted her uninjured hand and pounded it against his rock-hard shoulder.

"Dammit," she cried, "don't talk about me as if I weren't here,"

"I want to get her back to Dallas as quickly as possible, Tom."

"Sure. I understand."

"Did you hear me? I am right here, I am perfectly capable of—"

"I left my plane at a little airstrip outside Notrees," Cade said. "Do you know it?"

Tom nodded. "No problem, boss."

Boss, Angelica thought bitterly, *boss*! The foreman who'd done his best to ignore her all these months was doing everything but clicking his heels for Cade.

And to think, for a few brief moments when she'd recovered consciousness in that examining room, she'd almost felt grateful toward this man. She had a half-remembered vision of herself lying in his arms while he sucked the venom from her flesh, a memory of his voice, demanding that Tom find a way to make the truck go faster. And she'd thought she could still hear his tender whisper telling her that she would be fine, that he would not permit anything to happen to her.

Apparently, scorpion venom could cause hallucinations!

Angelica shut her eyes. "I hate you, Cade Landon," she said. She'd meant to shout the words at him but they came out a choked whisper. "I *hate* you," she said again.

Cade looked at the woman in his arms. Her hair was a tangle of copper silk, her blouse was dirty, her right arm was in a sling, and a glimmer of dampness was on her forehead.

She was a miserable-tempered, miserable-looking mess—and he needed to kiss her as badly as he needed to breathe.

In a day of illogical happenings, who was he to question yet another one?

"Hate me, then," he said, and he bent and touched his lips to hers.

He heard Tom's incredulous gasp, heard the same disbelief echoed in whatever it was Angelica started to say as his mouth took hers.

And then her free arm, the one that had been lying so stiffly around his neck, curved against his flesh. She gave a little shudder, not of fear but of something darker, and it sent an answering tremor racing through Cade's blood.

He drew her closer to him, reveling in the feel of her body turning soft and warm in his arms, in the way her mouth trembled and opened to his.

"Uh, boss?" Tom's dry gulp was audible in the stillness. "We're, uh, we're here. At the Notrees airstrip."

Cade blinked. He drew back, looked into Angelica's face, watched as the sweep of dark lashes fanning her cheeks slowly lifted.

She stared at him in silence, her eyes blurred with confusion. Then she stiffened in his arms and fixed him with a look the Medusa would have envied. It was only luck that kept him from turning to stone.

"I was right about you," she whispered. "You truly are a contemptible bastard."

Cade wanted to deny it—but, at the moment, he could only agree.

CHAPTER SIX

As soon as they boarded the Apache, Angelica surprised Cade by opening the vial of pain tablets and gulping two of them down.

"Does your hand hurt?"

"No," she said in a voice that dripped icicles, "it does not hurt. I took the pills because I had nothing better to do, and I thought they might be fun."

He looked at her in the faint light of the instrument panel and gave her a smile that more than matched the chill in her words.

"I'll be satisfied if they keep you quiet," he said.

And she was quiet. By the time they were airborne, her head was drooping back against the seat. Out of the corner of his eye, he saw her blink, then yawn. Within seconds, she was asleep.

Cade sighed and felt his muscles begin to relax. He loved flying, especially at night. He'd always found a star-filled sky the best place to think about whatever might be on his mind.

Tonight, what was on his mind—what wouldn't go away—was what had happened when they'd pulled up beside the plane.

Why in hell had he kissed her? It made no sense.

A contemptible bastard, she'd called him.

"Damn," he muttered in the darkness of the cockpit.

"Contemptible" was surely not the way a man wanted to think of himself. It was definitely not the way he wanted to be described by a woman, even when that woman was Angelica Gordon.

Even worse was the nagging realization that she was right.

He looked at Angelica again, lying curled beside him in sleep. She looked soft, and vulnerable, and almost painfully feminine—which only showed how deceiving looks could be. She was none of those things—or was she? He had tasted the softness of her lips, seen the sudden vulnerability in her eyes, felt the ripeness of her rounded breasts and hips....

He thumped the control wheel with his hand.

"Dammit, Landon!" he growled.

What kind of nonsense was this? There was nothing about Angelica Gordon that appealed to him. She was the very antithesis of what he liked a woman to be; what's more, she brought out the very worst in him, a strange, primitive desire to subdue and conquer.

For the first time in his life, he understood why a caveman might have hit a woman over the head, then dragged her off to his lair to prove, once and for all, which of them was the master—and, suddenly, it came to him.

He was not contemptible at all. He was desperate, as desperate as any man would be when pushed to the boundaries of sanity by a mean-tempered shrew.

Otherwise, why would he have confused the desire to throttle Angelica Gordon with the desire to kiss her?

And it was all Grant's fault. Grant was the one who'd sent him on this crazy mission, who'd urged him to move cautiously and discreetly, but then, his brother was a lawyer, and lawyers were notorious for making mountains out of molehills.

Cade's eyes narrowed. To hell with caution! It was time to trust his instincts.

It was time to call Angelica's bluff.

Either she produced proof to back up that verbal contract she'd boasted about or he'd smile, say goodbye and turn this entire mess over to the Landon legal eagles.

Let them sort it out. He was an oil man, not a detective, and he had things to do and places to see. He'd made it a point never to be tied to one place for too long and certainly not to one woman—and yet here he was, anchored to *this* place and *this* woman, and the worst of it was, he didn't care a damn about either!

London was waiting, and Dumai, where—where...

He frowned. What was that dancer's name, anyway? He couldn't remember. He couldn't even remember what she looked like.

But she was waiting, that was what mattered.

In the distance, he could see the white runway lights of the small airfield where this endless day had started. He began his descent, satisfied now that he'd decided upon a course of action.

All that remained was to get the incapacitated, sleeping woman beside him home and into bed.

And into bed... The thought sent a rush of heat curling through his blood. He could see himself taking her in his arms, carrying her up the stairs into darkness, then slowly stripping away her clothes.

Contemptible, he thought.

No, a voice inside him whispered, not contemptible. Insane. Staying in this city, dealing with Angelica—the whole thing was crazy.

Goodbye, Dallas, he thought. Goodbye, Angelica Gordon.

And then—hello, sanity.

If he could have patted himself on the back, he'd have done it. Instead, he settled for grinning foolishly at the fast-approaching runway.

Angelica yawned, stretched—and caught her breath.

Her hand, and her arm, hurt like the dickens.

Frowning, she struggled to get her bearings. She was in a vehicle—a pickup truck—racing swiftly through the night. And beside her, driving it, was the Hero of the Odessa oil fields, Mr. Cade Landon.

She put her uninjured hand to her hair and shoved the tangled mass from her face. If Cade was driving, they must be in Dallas. Yes. She could remember getting

into the truck outside the hospital, remember the ride
to the Notrees airstrip...

... remember Cade taking her in his arms and kissing
her, ignoring her protests, her pleas, her anger—

But not her breathless surrender.

She shuddered. Disgusting! How could she have re-
sponded to a kiss from that insufferable man? And he
was insufferable, no doubt about it, and never mind the
movie-star good looks or the kisses that she knew were
meant to make such a fool of her.

Cade Landon was the most arrogant, egotistical male
she'd met in the entire state of Texas, and that was saying
a lot.

He'd humiliated her in front of her banker and her
business associates, embarrassed her in front of her crew,
made her look like a fool in front of the staff of the
hospital—and why? Because she was female, and that
made her a lesser creature.

Her father had treated her mother the same way. Oh,
he'd claimed he was just being protective and loving,
but Angelica could still remember how her mother had
chafed and fumed. Who could have blamed her? No
intelligent woman would let herself be treated as if she
were a well-trained, obedient dog.

Men understood how to deal with women back
East. But here— Angelica's lip curled. Here, in Cade
Landon's world, they were too busy being macho to
figure out what a woman wanted.

Well, she'd had it! She wasn't up to a confrontation
tonight but tomorrow she was going to do what she
should have done from day one, she was going to stand
up to Cade Landon and tell him that either he accepted
her right to head up Gordon Oil or—or...

Or what? Or she'd see him in court? Landon
Enterprises probably had a trillion lawyers on retainer.
They probably had another trillion dollars to spend dis-
puting her claim.

She had nobody on retainer, not even a cleaning service, as Cade had so generously pointed out. And the last time she'd checked, she had exactly fifty-three dollars and eighty-four cents in her checking account—

"Are you awake?"

Angelica looked at Cade. His eyes were on the road.

"Of course I'm awake," she snapped. "Why?"

He shot her a quick, humorless smile. "Just checking. You slept straight through the flight from Notrees."

"I pretended to sleep," she said, tossing the hair from her eyes. "It was preferable to being forced to endure your company."

"You sure had me fooled, sugar. If I'd known that, I wouldn't have carried you to the truck."

Angelica flushed but said nothing. Had he carried her to the truck? He must have, because she certainly didn't remember walking. Now that she thought about it, she did remember the brush of his hand across her breasts as he unfastened her belt, the feel of his arms as they swept around her and lifted her...

"How do you feel?"

Awful. Her hand hurt, and her arm, and, now that she thought about it, so did her head.

"Fine," she said coldly.

"Maybe you ought to take another couple of pills."

"Maybe you ought to mind your business."

"That suits me." He looked at her and smiled tightly. "In fact, it suits me so well that I won't ask if you need anything from that all-night market on the corner up ahead."

Angelica bit down on her lip. Of course, she needed things. She hadn't shopped in days, hadn't even thought of it, to tell the truth, because she'd been so caught up in the disaster Cade Landon had brought down on her head.

She opened her mouth to say that she'd changed her mind, that she needed some frozen dinners, so she wouldn't have to worry about cooking while her hand healed, that she was out of tea and coffee and bread and that, given the way she felt right now, the odds of her getting out to shop on her own ranged from slim to nonexistent.

On the other hand, it would be better to starve than ask Cade for help.

"The only thing I need," she said, "is to be in my own house and to see the last of you."

"My thoughts precisely," Cade said, and pulled into her driveway.

Angelica fumbled at her seat belt with her left hand. "Thank you for your help," she said in a way that made the words a lie.

"You're welcome," he said, his tone as sarcastic as hers. Then he doused the headlights, turned off the engine and got out of the truck.

"What are you doing?" she said as he came around to her door and opened it.

"I'm seeing you in."

"I don't need anyone to see me in."

Cade tipped back his Colorado Rockies baseball cap. "No?" he said pleasantly.

"No," she said, not so pleasantly.

He laughed softly. "The way it looks to me, sugar, you need somebody just to see you out of this truck."

It was true, unfortunately. It was one thing to open a seat belt one-handed, but now she was having trouble grasping the door frame for leverage, and she was feeling too unsteady to risk simply dropping the short distance to the ground without hanging on to something.

"What do you say, sugar? Shall I help you?"

Angelica glared at him. "Yes," she said through her teeth.

"Yes, what?"

"Dammit, Cade, this isn't funny!"

He reached into the cab of the truck, gathered her into his arms and shouldered the door closed. "You know," he said, as he started across the narrow strip of lawn, "I've been thinking—"

"I can see the headlines now," Angelica said sweetly. " 'Cade Landon thinks!' "

"I've been thinking," he continued without missing a beat, "that I must have the wrong idea about that fancy school you teach in."

"I don't teach there," she said stiffly. Was it possible to loop your arm around a man's neck, to feel his arms around you and pretend none of it was happening? "I'm a careers counselor. And I've no doubt you have the wrong idea about Miss Palmer's. It's not fancy, it's simply a place where young women can learn in an atmosphere conducive to the development of their full potential."

Cade chuckled as he mounted the porch steps. "Meaning, no boys allowed?"

"Miss Palmer's is gender exclusive, yes."

"Tell me something, sugar. How can you spout such nonsense and still toss off so many dammits?"

Angelica frowned. "It's not nonsense. And I don't—"

"Yeah, you do. For a lady who probably drinks her tea with her pinky stuck out, you sure curse a lot."

Her cheeks reddened. "Perhaps it's because I was unfortunate enough to have spent my early years in Texas."

"And that's something else I don't understand." Cade lowered her to the porch floor. "If you despise Texas, why did you come back?"

"I don't despise Texas," Angelica said. A frown creased her forehead. Standing on her own, her legs felt amazingly wobbly. She reached back and grasped the porch railing for support. "I just think that anyplace where time stands still is unappealing. And you know why I came back. To run Gordon Oil."

"To run it into the ground, you mean."

"I have not run it into the ground. The company wasn't in good shape before, and—and..." Lord, she felt shaky. She took a breath and tried for a nonchalant shrug. "It's late, and you already have all the answers. So good night, and—"

"And thank you for your help. Yes, I know." He stuck out his hand. "Keys, please."

"What?"

"You heard me. I want your house keys."

"Why?"

"Because I'm not leaving until I've seen you safely inside."

Their eyes met, and Angelica stiffened with anger at what she saw in his, the steely determination and masculine arrogance.

It was obvious that saying no wouldn't get her very far.

Gritting her teeth, she dug her left hand into her pocket, pulled out the keys and dropped them into his outstretched palm.

"Fine. Go ahead, Cade. Open the door. I can see we're going to have to go through this 'Me Tarzan, you Jane' charade or I'll never get rid of you!"

"Clever girl."

"Clever woman." Her chin lifted in defiance. "There's a difference."

To her surprise, he laughed. "OK, *woman*," he said, "let's get you tucked away for the night."

She didn't argue as he swung her into his arms again. Arguing with him was useless; besides, she had the awful feeling she might fall down if she tried to get through the door on her own, and heaven only knew how she'd get rid of him then.

Angelica frowned as he stepped into the darkened entry hall and kicked the door shut after him. What had he meant, tucked away for the night? There was a ring to that phrase that she didn't much—

"Where's the light switch?"

"On the wall, to the right, but you needn't—"

She blinked in the sudden glare as the overhead light blazed on.

"You can put me down now," she said, "and thank you for—"

"Did you know that you have a way of making 'thank you' sound like an insult?" Cade shifted her in his arms and looked at the narrow, sharply inclined staircase rising ahead. "Where's your bedroom? Upstairs?"

"Will you put me down? I am perfectly capable of—"

"Of walking those steps?" He shook his head. "I don't think so."

Well, no. She wasn't and she knew it. With luck, she hoped she might be able to make it to the love seat in the living room—not the best place to spend the night, considering her height and the love seat's length, but—

"Angelica," Cade said, "I'm going to ask you one more time. Where is your bedroom? And before you decide I only want to know so I can have my evil way with you, let me assure you that all I want is to see you safely to bed so I can get the hell out of here and back to my hotel where maybe, just maybe, I can sit down at the bar and have a steak and fries and a bourbon and branch water in peace."

"In peace—with some woman, no doubt!"

What on earth had made her say that? But Cade didn't seem to notice. He simply went on glaring at her until finally she puffed out her breath.

"Upstairs. First door on the right."

"Thank you very much," he said coldly.

She turned her face from his as he made his way up the stairs. So, he was as eager to get rid of her as she was to get rid of him. That was a comfort.

But it wasn't a comfort to imagine him sitting in some cozy pub while some smiling blonde with a large chest and a tiny brain hung on his every word.

"—the right room?"

Angelica swallowed hard. "I—I'm sorry," she said, "did you—did you ask me something?"

"I said, is this the right room?"

"I—uh..." She looked around her, then nodded. "Yes, this is it. The light's there, on the table beside the bed."

Cade carried her to the bed, put her down, then turned on the light. He straightened up and glanced around him.

The room was small, he saw, and the bed narrow. It must have been Angelica's when she was a girl.

"I suppose it's time to thank you again," she said.

He laughed and looked at her. "Even if it'll kill you to do it," he said—and frowned.

Damn! The woman had kept him so busy arguing that he hadn't really taken a good look at her in hours. Now that he did, what he saw was disconcerting.

Her eyes were smudged with fatigue and almost sunken into her head. Her face had taken on a white, pinched look; even her mouth, that soft, rosebud mouth, was drained of color.

He looked at her hands, lying in her lap. The bandaged one was obviously swollen; the other was trembling.

Cade felt as if someone had just sunk a fist into his belly. She wasn't just tired, she was exhausted—or worse.

"Angelica." She looked up, and he could see the effort the simple action cost her. "Angelica," he said, sounding fierce and angry, "are you ill?"

"I'm fine," she said quickly. Too quickly, he thought, and he reached down and gripped her shoulders.

"No games," he said, his eyes on hers. "Just tell me the truth. Are you feeling sick?"

She hesitated, and then she sighed. What was there to gain by lying?

"Not sick," she said. "I just—I feel tired. More than tired. And my head hurts. My hand, too, and my arm..." She looked at him and gave a shaky laugh. "Is that truthful enough for you?"

A muscle knotted in his cheek. "Yes," he said grimly, "it is."

"All I need is a night's sleep . . . Hey!" Her voice rose as Cade began undoing the buttons on her blouse. "Hey, what are you doing?"

"You're the one with two university degrees," he said tightly. "Figure it out for yourself." She slapped at his hands but he ignored her. One by one, the buttons slipped from their holes. "Let me tell you something, sugar. This may come as a shock—hell, maybe it's going to be a disappointment—but I am not a man who's turned on by women who look as if they're about to pass out."

"I'm not . . ." She frowned. "Is that—is that how I look?"

Cade smiled tightly. "To be precise, you look like something the cat dragged in. Give me your left arm, please." She did, and the blouse slid from her shoulder. "Can you move your right arm at all?" Her sudden intake of breath provided all the answer he needed. "Just sit still, then, and let me—OK. Now, lift your leg."

"Cade, really, you don't have to undress me!"

"Somebody has to," he growled as he undid her laces and yanked off her shoes. "And I don't see any ladies-in-waiting hovering in the background."

"Yes, but—"

"But what?" He lifted angry eyes to her face. "Are you going to tell me you'll be able to unzip your jeans or get them off?" He smiled grimly at her silence. "Exactly. Now, lie back, please, and stop arguing."

Stop arguing? Angelica would have laughed, but she didn't have the energy. Arguing was useless. Cade had already tilted her onto the bed, already reached for the snap at her waist. His touch was deft and impersonal, but she closed her eyes anyway.

This was not how she'd imagined Cade Landon undressing her, she thought.

Her eyes snapped open. She hadn't thought of him undressing her at all—or had she?

"Lift up," he said. His face might have been carved of stone, for all the expression it wore.

Dutifully, she raised her hips while he slid down her jeans and tugged them off, leaving her in a white cotton camisole, white cotton panties and heavy wool socks.

A truly alluring outfit, she thought. Not that it mattered. If Cade Landon were the last man on earth, she wouldn't—she couldn't—

Oh, God, she thought, and a tremor raced through her.

"Angelica?" She looked at him. The expression on his face had changed, become puzzled.

"I—I'm OK." Say something, she told herself, say anything. "I—I have to go to the bathroom."

Cade smiled a little. "Sorry. I should have thought of that. OK, put your arm around my neck and—"

"No! I mean—I can do that much without help!"

"But you'll need help to get there," he said, and lifted her into his arms. "Which way?"

Which way? Which way, indeed? My God, what was happening to her? This man—this contemptible man—was holding her all but naked body in his arms, she hated him and he hated her, and yet—and yet, the desire to bring his mouth down to hers, to spread her hand over his chest and feel the beat of his heart, was almost more than she could endure.

"Angelica," he said impatiently, "where's the bathroom?"

The bathroom, she thought, the bathroom.

"It's—it's just down the hall."

He nodded, his expression blank, and carried her into the corridor. It was all she could do to keep from burying her face in his shoulder for fear he might read in her eyes what was happening to her, the hot, sharp waves of desire that were curling through her bones.

She was almost breathless by the time he put her down inside the white-tiled room.

"I'll be just outside," he said, and switched on the light. Then he smiled reassuringly, shut the door after him—and groaned softly into the silence.

Damn! Maybe he really was contemptible. Maybe he was the no-good bastard Angelica Gordon thought he was.

No, he thought, and took a deep, deep breath, no, if he were really that, he'd have acted on the sudden, intoxicating desire that had almost driven him to his knees, he'd have stripped away that silly, virginal camisole, the cotton panties, the sweat socks—he'd have stripped off that whole idiotic outfit and made love to Angelica until she lay trembling in his arms.

How could he have felt that way? Undressing her had been a purely mechanical act, one he hadn't thought about except in terms of how to best do it efficiently, without hurting her injured hand.

And then, when he'd finished, he'd looked at her as she lay there in that sexless getup and all of a sudden he'd felt as if the breath were being sucked out of his lungs.

He'd wanted to kiss the weariness from her eyes, to kiss her lips until they were pink again. He'd wanted to stroke the smooth inch of belly that he glimpsed under the hem of the camisole....

He sighed, lifted his hands to his face and massaged his temples. Forget the bourbon. Forget everything but a hot shower or, better still, a cold one and then a good, sound night's rest.

Sleep was what he needed, sleep and a ticket on the first plane out of Dallas—

The bathroom door swung open. Cade turned around. Angelica was standing in the doorway.

"I'm finished," she said—and all at once, to his horror, tears rose in her eyes and rolled down her cheeks.

"Sugar," he said, clasping her shoulders, "what is it?"

"I—I just got a look at myself in the mirror," she sobbed, and raised tearstained lashes to him. "You're right, Cade, I look like hell."

He stared at her for a long moment and then he laughed and swept her into his arms.

"I lied," he said as he carried her into the bedroom. "You're beautiful."

For some reason, the flippant answer made her angry.

"Don't treat me like a fool," she snapped. "I know I'm not!"

He grinned as he whipped back the blankets and deposited her gently beneath them.

"OK, then you're not."

"Cade, dammit—"

He leaned forward, captured her face in his hands and kissed her gently on the mouth.

"Do you want to hear the truth?" he said, his lips an inch from hers. "I don't think I've ever seen a more beautiful woman than you, sugar."

Her lips parted, but before she could speak he kissed her again. His hand threaded into her hair, held it wrapped like a copper flame around his wrist. His mouth opened over hers and the tip of his tongue brushed against her lips.

Angelica made a soft sound of pleasure. Her eyes closed, her lips parted, and her fingers curled into his shirt.

Cade groaned softly. He touched his mouth to her earlobe, then left a trail of warm kisses along her flesh until he reached the hollow of her throat. His hand slid up her ribs, moved under the cotton camisole. He felt her tremble and he whispered her name and cupped her naked breast in his palm.

His brain was shrieking out a message, but his body wasn't listening. It was hardening, aching with the need to possess this soft, sweet-smelling woman, this Angelica who burned like fire in his arms.

He sat down on the bed beside her, sliding his hand over her belly, over the foolish cotton panties, and he cupped her through the soft fabric.

Angelica groaned and strained toward him, her mouth open and hungry, her arm winding around his neck.

Sensation after sensation swept over her, each electrifying. The feel of Cade's mouth moving against hers, and the taste. The stroke of his fingers against her nipple. And oh, the heat of his hand moving between her thighs, the weight of it pressing against her so that she was suddenly flooded with dampness.

"Sweet," he whispered, "sweet Angelica."

She whispered his name, reached up to him, took his face in her hands...

And cried out in pain.

Cade sprang back. He stared into her flushed face, into her stunned eyes.

My God, he thought, what am I doing? What kind of man took advantage of a woman groggy from medication?

He hadn't meant to take advantage, hadn't even meant to kiss her.

"I'm sorry," he said, "I didn't mean to..." He drew the blanket to her chin. "Are you all right?"

She wasn't, she thought, she wasn't all right. How could she be, to have let herself be carried away like that? It had to be the medicine, and exhaustion.

"Angelica?"

"Yes," she lied, "I'm fine." She took a deep breath. "Cade, it's been a long day, and the medicine... I think— I think it's time you left."

"All right." He rose from the bed. "But I don't think you should be alone for a while. Suppose I go downstairs and call Emily? I'm sure she'll be happy to stay with you for a couple of days."

"No, I don't need—" She hesitated. There was no point in pretending. What had just happened was proof that it was all catching up to her, the stress and the pain, and with a little shrug of her shoulders, she gave in. "OK. Maybe you're right. Her number is tacked to the wall next to the phone in the kitchen."

Outside, in the hallway, he took a deep breath, cursed himself for being seven times a fool and decided that his decision to leave Dallas had been a very wise one.

Whatever had happened in that bedroom just now only proved that when you reached overload, anything was possible.

He found Emily's number and dialed it and, as her phone rang, he tried to concentrate on the woman waiting in Dumai instead of the one lying in that narrow bed upstairs.

What was her name? What did she look like? It upset him that he couldn't remember. He frowned. Exhaustion was clearly catching up to him.

"Come on," he muttered, as the phone rang and rang. What was taking so long? The tiny rooms and narrow staircase of this little house were threatening to crush him.

Finally, a voice croaked brokenly in his ear.

"Hullo?"

"Emily?" he said, puzzled.

"Mr. Landon? Is that you?"

"Yes, it's me. Emily, what's wrong? You sound terrible."

"I *feel* terrible, Mr. Landon. I've got the flu."

Cade closed his eyes. It never rains but it pours, he thought wearily. No, he said calmly, no, he hadn't called about anything terribly important. He'd just—he'd just...

Hastily, he improvised, offering a barely coherent reason for his phone call. Not that it mattered. Emily was too sick to notice. She wasn't going to be at work for the next several days, she said, and apologized for the inconvenience.

"No problem," Cade said cheerfully.

He hung up the phone and ran his fingers through his hair. Now what? He'd thought he could simply put Angelica to bed and walk out, but he'd been kidding himself. She needed someone.

A home nursing service. Yes, maybe that would do it—but he wouldn't be able to reach one at this hour.

Perhaps she had a friend who could come stay with her. A woman? A man? Was there a man in her life?

Cade's jaw clenched. It was none of his business what she did or who she did it with. Why should the thought make him so angry? Because he was tired and hungry, that's why, he thought grimly. Well, at least he could solve part of that problem.

He got to his feet, went into the kitchen, yanked open the refrigerator door and peered inside.

There was a lump of something unidentifiable, a heel of bread on its way to becoming penicillin and a carton of yogurt. The cupboards yielded little more except the knowledge that if he wanted a cup of coffee, or tea, or even cocoa, he was in trouble.

Cade was scowling as he headed up the stairs to Angelica's room.

"Angelica," he said severely—and fell silent.

She was fast asleep, lying as he had left her, looking as forlorn as anything he'd ever seen. He made a move toward the bed, his hand lifting as if to smooth down the covers, but then he took a step back.

"This is ridiculous," he muttered to her sleeping form. "Why didn't they keep you in that hospital overnight?"

Not that she'd have stayed if they'd suggested it, he thought. She'd have insisted she was perfectly capable of taking care of herself.

With a groan, he sank down in the old-fashioned rocking chair opposite the bed and lay his head back.

Now what? he thought.

It was a good question. A very good question. The trouble was, he had no answers.

Cade closed his eyes. Seconds later, he was asleep.

CHAPTER SEVEN

ANGELICA stirred as the morning sun cast its bright light across her face.

She sighed, murmured something unintelligible and turned her face to the side, but the light wouldn't go away. Frowning, she threw her arm over her face to shield her eyes—

And came swiftly awake.

Pain shot through her arm, radiating sharply from her hand to her shoulder. She gave a hiss of distress, struggled up against the pillows—and gaped in astonishment at what she saw.

Cade was sound asleep, sprawled in the old rocking chair near her bed. His long legs were stretched out in front of him and crossed at the ankles, his head lolled back against the headrest at an angle that had to be uncomfortable. The chair, too small for his bulk, might have made another man look foolish.

It only made Cade look more blatantly masculine.

Angelica swallowed dryly, then ran the tip of her tongue over her lips. Automatically, the fingers of her left hand closed around the edge of the blanket and she drew it to her chin.

What was Cade doing here? Last night's memories were blurred. Damn those horrible pain pills! She could recall only bits and pieces of the flight from Notrees and the drive to the house, and things were hardly clearer after that—Cade carrying her into the house, then up the steps to her bedroom; Cade undressing her...

Angelica blushed. It had been embarrassing—but not humiliating. Cade had been so gentle, so matter-of-fact about taking off her clothing. He'd been careful of both her injured hand and her sensibilities, something she'd never have expected from a man like him.

But there was another memory, a disquieting one.

Cade putting her to bed. Cade taking her in his arms and kissing her. The heat of his mouth, and the heat of his hands as they'd moved on her flesh, the way he'd held her and touched her and awakened a fire in her so hot its flames should have consumed her.

Angelica closed her eyes, wishing desperately she could forget and knowing that she couldn't. Her wildly uninhibited response to him was so crazy, so unlike what she...

It must have had something to do with the medication she'd taken.

A soft moan of despair rose in her throat and she fell back against the pillows.

Who was she kidding? It hadn't been the medicine any more than it had been the medicine that had awakened her at dawn from a dream so erotic that it had left her breathless—and he'd been right here, while she'd been dreaming of him, sprawled in a chair not five feet away.

The realization was disturbing, although she wasn't quite sure why. All she knew was that Cade Landon had turned out to be an intruder not just in her life but in her dreams and now in her bedroom, and she didn't like it.

"Enough," she said grimly, and shoved aside the bedclothes.

She got to her feet, wincing at the pain that ricocheted through her arm. Left-handed, she yanked the blanket from the bed and whisked it around herself like a toga. Then she stalked to the rocking chair and glared at Cade's peacefully sleeping form.

"Cade," she said sharply. He didn't move. Angelica moved closer, her mouth thinned with anger. "Dammit, wake up!"

When he still didn't move, she punctuated the demand by bending down and jabbing her uninjured fist into his mid-section.

Cade shot upright in the chair. Where in hell was he? What was the apparition standing over him? The light was almost blinding him; all he could make out was a tall figure wrapped up like an Egyptian mummy, its head enshrouded in a nimbus of flame...

He groaned. It was Angelica.

Cade scrubbed his hands over his face. Had he really fallen asleep in this miserable chair? His whole body ached from the experience. And the sight of Angelica standing over him, looking more like an avenging angel than a woman recovering from a scorpion sting, did not suggest that the day was off to a pleasant start.

"Angelica," he said in a sleep-roughened voice.

"Cade," she said. Her voice bore an Arctic chill.

He looked up at her, ran his fingers through his tousled hair and tried a good-morning smile.

"What time is it?"

"Time for you to get out of my bedroom."

Cade sighed. So much for starting the day off with a smile, he thought, and got to his feet.

"What are you doing in my bedroom, Cade? The last I heard, Emily was coming to stay the night."

"Right," he said, still struggling to get his bearings. "How does your hand feel this morning?"

"My hand is my business. Answer the question, please. What are you doing in my bedroom?"

He looked at her. Her color was better than it had been last night but there was a tight look to her mouth that suggested she was still in pain.

"Look," he said, "if it hurts, just say so. I can go down and get you an ice pack or—"

"I repeat, how I feel is my business, not yours. Where is Emily?"

A muscle knotted in Cade's jaw. "I don't do very well at question and answer games until after I've at least splashed cold water on my face,'' he said, trying hard to control his temper. "Do you think you could give me five minutes before the inquisition begins?"

Angelica took a step back. "Five minutes," she said unsmilingly. "Not a minute more."

He made his way past her, taking his time about it just to annoy her as he walked down the hall and into the bathroom. Once the door shut after him, he leaned his hands on the sink and glowered at his reflection in the mirror.

"Thank you for staying with me last night, Cade," he muttered in an unkind parody of Angelica's voice, "and thank you for spending the night on the rack just so I wouldn't be alone."

He made a face at himself. Angelica, offering him thanks? Only a fool would expect it. Besides, he hadn't really planned on spending the night. The last thing he remembered, he'd sat down in that miserable chair—

And apparently gone out like a light. Well, he thought as he turned away from the sink, it didn't matter. The decision he'd reached last night seemed more valid than ever. He was going to call Angelica's bluff. And when she had to admit that she had nothing to back it up, he'd smile politely, tell her his lawyers would be in touch and wave goodbye.

Thinking of that would help him stay cool, no matter how she provoked him.

She wanted to act as if he'd committed a crime by spending the night contorted by that chair? Fine. Let her.

She wanted to pretend her hand was fine? OK. He'd pretend, too.

She was right. What happened to her was not his business.

Cade flushed the toilet, turned to the sink and splashed water on his bristly face. A toothbrush, he thought, three aspirin, and I'll feel like a new man.

He looked at the medicine cabinet. The efficient Angelica might keep a spare toothbrush in it; at the very least, she'd have a bottle of aspirin.

In fact, there were a couple of brushes, still snugly sealed in their plastic containers. He took one, opened it, drew a line of toothpaste across the bristles and began brushing his teeth.

When he'd almost finished, he paused, looked into the mirror and frowned. Why did she have those extra brushes? Was it a matter of efficiency—or was it in case she had overnight guests? Male guests, for instance.

Cade swung the cabinet door open again. She had a neat little stack of disposable razors on the shelf, too, which might be meant for shaving her legs—those long, shapely legs he'd gotten such a close look at last night—but then again, she might keep them for overnight visitors who...

He swore under his breath, rinsed his mouth and tossed the toothbrush into the wastebasket. She could have hordes of men trotting through, he didn't give a damn. He laughed to himself as he pictured them, round-shouldered, effete snobs with pasty skins and delicate hands. So what? What did it matter to him?

He peered into the cabinet again, ignoring the neatly arranged razors, looking instead for the aspirin. Angelica didn't seem to believe in aspirin. She believed, instead, in vitamins, a deodorant in a surprisingly feminine vial and at least four different kinds of something called hair gel.

Cade took down one of the containers and studied the label.

"'Guaranteed to tame problem hair,'" he read aloud.

What problem hair? Her hair was glorious; even last night, when it had been spread across the pillows in an uncombed tangle, he'd been struck by the wild beauty of it....

He cursed again, shoved the container into the cabinet and slammed the door.

Coffee, he thought firmly, that's what he needed next, and he already knew there was none in the house. Well, that store they'd passed last night must have some. He'd phone, arrange for a delivery. Coffee, and orange juice, bacon and eggs and bread. And a giant-size bottle of aspirin.

Then he'd call a nursing service, make arrangements and say goodbye to Dallas and Angelica Gordon.

The thought made his day.

Smiling, he opened the bathroom door and stepped out into the hall. The house was very quiet. Had Angelica gone back to bed? He hoped so. The less he saw of her from this point on, the better.

Cade's nostrils dilated. What was that smell? It was drifting up the stairway, sharp and almost acrid. By God, something was burning!

His heart started to pound. He raced into Angelica's bedroom, saw that it was empty, turned and charged down the stairs.

"Angelica?" he roared. "Angelica!"

He reached the kitchen on a run. The smoke was thick enough to make him gag; it was belching from a toaster that was in the process of immolating itself.

Angelica lay sprawled on the floor.

Fear clawed at Cade's throat. He yanked the plug from the wall, grabbed the toaster between two dish towels, ran to the back door and slung the burning toaster out onto the cement patio. Then he raced to where Angelica lay.

"Sugar," he whispered, and knelt down beside her. She was sobbing, and his heart turned over. Gently, he clasped her shoulders and drew her to him, "what is it? Did you get burned? Angelica, please, talk to..."

His words trailed off. She wasn't sobbing, she was panting—panting with anger and with frustration as she struggled to free herself from the blanket that lay tangled around her.

"This miserable thing," she huffed, "this awful, horrible thing!"

Cade took a deep breath. He counted to ten, then rose and drew her up beside him. The blanket fell to the floor and he bent down, grabbed it and wrapped it around her shoulders with hands that were none too gentle.

"OK," he said through his teeth, "let's have it. What happened?"

"What do you mean, what happened?" She flung him a look of pure defiance and clutched the blanket to her breasts with her good hand. "The bread started to burn, so I tried to get it out of the toaster. But I couldn't reach it with my left hand, and then, when I tried to turn around, this—this stupid blanket got caught under my feet and—and..."

"Let me get this straight." Cade folded his arms across his chest and looked at her. "First, you came down that narrow flight of steps with a blanket trailing under your feet. When you didn't trip over the blanket and break your neck, you figured what the hell, why not go for broke? So you came in here, turned on the toaster—"

"Don't be ridiculous!" Angelica tossed her head so that her mane of wild curls tumbled down her back. She turned, stalked away from him, then swung to face him again. The hem of the blanket swirled around her bare feet. "I came down to have breakfast and I tripped. End of story. You're making much more out of this than it deserves."

"Really?" He put his hands on his hips. "Suppose I hadn't been here? Suppose there'd been no one to help you? Suppose the house had gone up in flames?"

"That wouldn't have happened."

"No?"

"No. All I did was burn some bread, and—"

"All you did was set the toaster on fire! As for the bread—" Cade swung away and yanked open the refrigerator door. "What bread are we talking about? You can't mean that laboratory experiment in mold growth I saw last night!"

Angelica took a step toward him, her eyes blazing. "Don't you dare yell at me, Cade Landon!"

"If you're going to act like a damned fool, I have every right to yell! What were you doing down here in the first place? You're supposed to be upstairs, in your bed."

"Says who?"

Cade's lips twisted. "The man who was with you when the scorpion stung you, who watched you collapse, who knows how woozy you were last night, *that's* who!"

"I was flying on those pills last night. Besides, none of that gives you the right to—to bully me!"

He reached out and caught her by the shoulders. There was a dangerous glint in his eyes as he hauled her toward him.

"You know something, sugar? You keep accusing me of being a bully and I'm just liable to show you what a real bully is."

"Don't threaten me," she said furiously. "I don't like it."

"Then listen to reason! Trying to pretend you're fine when you're not isn't very bright, and neither is traipsing around in a blanket when you're not steady on your feet."

"Oh, for God's sake!" Angelica twisted away from him. "Don't you think I thought of that? I tried to get my robe on, but—"

"But you couldn't." Her silence was all the answer he needed. "Dammit," he growled, "why didn't you ask me for help?"

"Because—because..." Because I don't need your help, she thought, because I resent being dependent on you—because I remember all too vividly how it felt to be undressed and in your arms....

"Well? Why didn't you call me?"

Angelica moistened her lips. "You're just ticked off because I didn't tell you I was going to come downstairs."

"Tell me?"

"That's right, tell you that I was going downstairs to make my own breakfast in my own house!" She blew a stray curl off her forehead. "That's what this is all about and you know it. You just can't deal with a woman who can do for herself."

"What I can't deal with is a woman who's determined to behave like a damned fool."

She looked at him for a long moment and then she sighed.

"Look, I'm—grateful—for your assistance yesterday."

Cade laughed. "The word sticks in your throat, doesn't it?"

"Between the shock of the scorpion sting," she said, ignoring the interruption, "and the effect of those pills, I wasn't much good for anything. But now—"

"But now," he said, "it's time I got out of your way."

"Cade, please. I'm trying to be polite, but—"

"Polite? You? Hell, you don't know the meaning of the word!"

Angelica's head came up. "Maybe you're right," she snapped. "But it's hard to be polite to a man who invites himself to spend the night in your bedroom and then won't tell you why."

"Try this on for size, sugar. I called Emily, found out she was sick with the flu, went up to tell that to you—and found you sound asleep. I sat down, tried to decide what to do next—and the next thing I knew, it was morning and you were doing everything but using a cattle prod to show me just how pleased you were to see me."

"Dammit, Cade..." Her breath caught. "Oh."

"Oh? That's it? Just, 'oh'? No apologies for being nasty or for the fact that spending the night in that chair left me twisted like a pretzel? Just..." Cade frowned. "What's wrong?" The oh had not been meant as a comment; one look at her pale face confirmed that. "Angelica." He clasped her shoulders and eased her into a chair. "What is it?"

"I—I hit my hand against the table," she said. Her smile was as shaky as her voice. "It's nothing. Really, I'm fine."

"Sure you are," he said grimly. "Suppose we stop squabbling and check out that hand of yours."

"It's fine."

"Let me be the judge of that."

"Cade, really—"

It was useless to protest. He was already moving the blanket from her shoulder, turning it aside and reaching for her hand. His fingers closed around her bandaged flesh with surprising gentleness. Frowning, he bent his head and began to unwind the gauze.

"Easy," he said softly. "I'm not going to hurt you. I just want to see how the wound looks this morning."

His voice droned on, soft and reassuring and yet firm as he knelt before her. Angelica looked down at the top of his head. His hair was uncombed, the thick, silky locks a dozen different shades of gold as the morning sun kissed it.

She felt her throat constrict. Wouldn't it be nice if she could press a kiss there, too? She could touch her nose to his hair, her lips to his neck...

His fingers moved lightly against her skin, grazing her wrist and the palm of her hand, and she made a little sound, something halfway between clearing her throat and catching her breath.

Cade looked up.

"Did I hurt you?"

Angelica shook her head. "No. No, not at all."

"I'm trying to be gentle. I just want to be sure you're not going to get an infection in the area of the sting."

"You are. Being gentle, I mean. And—and..." She pulled her hand free of his. "Really, Cade, I'm fine."

Oh, yes, he thought, his eyes narrowing as he looked at her, yes, she was fine. She was—hell, she was gorgeous, sitting there like that with her hair blazing around her face, with that dumb blanket folded back so it made a frame for her creamy shoulders. One of the camisole straps had slipped down her arm; before he could think, he reached out and put his fingers under it, lifted it carefully and drew it back onto her shoulder.

"Thank you," she murmured.

He smiled. "A real thank you," he said. "Who'd have believed it?"

Their eyes met. She hesitated, and then she smiled at him.

"I—I guess I haven't been very easy to deal with."

"No." His smile broadened. "No, you haven't."

She nodded. "The—the scorpion sting... It, ah, it scared me silly."

It was an incredible admission, coming from this woman. Cade knew it, and forced himself to react as casually as if she'd simply commented on the weather.

"Well, that's understandable. I've seen men twice your size spot one of those little monsters inside a boot and keel over in a dead faint."

Angelica laughed. God, it was a glorious sight, he thought, watching those green eyes light, seeing those soft rosebud lips part to show perfect white teeth.

"You're just saying that to make me feel better."

Cade put on his most innocent look, crossed his heart and held up his hand.

"Cross my heart and hope to die, join the ghosts up in the sky, it's the truth and not a lie—what are you laughing at?"

"Join the ghosts up in the sky?" Angelica giggled. "What kind of silly stuff is that?"

He grinned. "It's obvious you never ran across any members of the Deadeye Defenders."

"The what?"

"There were three of us. Zach was ten, Grant was twelve and I was eight."

"The Deadeyes didn't believe in age discrimination, I see."

Cade chuckled. "We couldn't. We're brothers, and that oath you just laughed at was sacred."

"No girls permitted in the Deadeye Defenders, of course."

"Oh, we let one girl join. Kyra. She was—I guess you'd say she was our mascot."

Angelica's brows arched. "Of course. What else would a girl be good for?"

"Pull back those claws, sugar." Cade grinned. "Kyra was our baby sister. She was toddling around in diapers when the Deadeyes began—she was lucky we tolerated her at all!"

"Ah. Well, in that case—"

"Don't tell me I'm going to get another apology?" Cade clamped his hand to his heart. "The shock might kill me."

She laughed softly. "Relax, Mr. Landon. I was only going to say I hoped that by the time she was older, you'd decided that sex discrimination was as pointless as age discrimination."

Cade's smile faded a little. "By the time she was older, my brothers and I were too busy for childish stuff like the Deadeyes. That was what my old man said, anyway."

"But your mother—didn't she..." Angelica caught her bottom lip between her teeth. "I'm sorry, Cade. I didn't mean to pry."

"No, that's OK. Our mother died when we were just kids. Our old man—my father—had his own ideas about how to raise us." Their eyes met. He cleared his throat, then reached for her hand again. "OK," he said briskly, "let's just see how this looks."

Angelica swallowed as she looked at his bent head. She could bury the fingers of her left hand in his hair, curl them around the nape of his neck and urge his face up until his eyes met hers, until his mouth was a breath from her own...

She yanked her hand from his. Cade looked up, startled.

"If that hurts—"

"It doesn't hurt," she said sharply. "I just—look, I hate to be fussed over. If—if my hand is all right, just say so."

"It's going to be fine. We'll leave it unbandaged. Of course, you can't do much with it for the next few days, but—"

Angelica pushed back her chair and stood up. "I'll be sure to keep your advice in mind. Now, if that's all—"

"You'll have to do more than keep it in mind." Cade rose to his feet, frowning. "If you abuse that hand, Angelica—"

"I've no intention of abusing it, I assure you."

"No. The nurse won't let you, even if you wanted to."

"Nurse? What nurse?"

"Do you have a phone directory? I'm sure it won't take me long to make arrangements."

"Dammit, Cade, what are you talking about?"

"Well, it's obvious you can't be on your own just yet. And I told you about Emily."

"So?" Angelica clasped the blanket at her right shoulder and looked at him.

"So," he said with a little smile, "I'm going to call an agency and hire someone to—"

"You will not!"

His smile tilted. "Angelica, don't be stubborn. We've agreed, you won't be yourself for a few days."

"We did not agree that I needed a baby-sitter!"

Cade put his hands on his hips. "That's nonsense! I'm simply trying to—"

"You just can't help yourself, can you? Any time the opportunity presents itself, you try to take over!"

"Angelica, dammit, don't be a fool."

Angelica lifted her head in defiance. "Goodbye, Cade. Thank you again for all your help. I'll be in touch."

He stared at her for a long moment and then he began to laugh. "*You'll* be in touch? Haven't you got our roles reversed here, lady? I'm the one who'll be in touch— when I need a report, or a file, or any one of a hundred things from that closet you call an office."

She flushed. "Thank you for reminding me that I'm only here to serve you, Mr. Landon. Don't worry. You'll get whatever you want when you want it."

Cade strolled across the room and looked out the door to the patio. The toaster was lying where he'd tossed it, blackened and dead. He swung toward Angelica, who was looking at him with all the disdain she could manage.

"How?" he said pleasantly, and smiled.

"How what?"

He tucked his hands into the back pockets of his jeans. "How will you see to it that I get whatever I need when I need it? Emily won't be at her desk, remember?"

She'd forgotten about Emily being out with the flu. But she didn't say that; she simply lifted her shoulders in a nonchalant shrug.

"I'll manage."

"How?" he repeated. "You're going to have to figure out a way to get yourself dressed, and showered, and fed, and to work. I don't suppose your car is an automatic, is it?"

She flushed again. "Suppose you get to the point."

The point, he thought, as he looked at her. What in hell *was* the point?

He'd made up his mind to put an end to the game, to demand proof of the supposed verbal contract between her father and his, then get out of here and let Landon Enterprises' legal staff do its work, but—but...

He took a deep breath. "Here's the point," he said brusquely, taking her elbow and herding her toward the stairs. She tried to pull free but he held on to her so that she had no choice but to let him lead her up the steps with him. "You're right about it being nonsense for me to hire a nurse."

They reached the landing, and now he was leading her to her bedroom.

"Well," she said crisply, "I'm glad you've come to your senses. Of course it would be nonsense. I don't need a nurse."

"Exactly. What you need is to be in a situation that's convenient for the both of us."

"I agree. And..." She spun toward him as they stepped into the bedroom. "What do you mean, convenient for both of us?"

Cade pulled open the door to the wardrobe and peered inside. "My God," he said, shaking his head, "it looks as if you've cornered the market in tweed!"

Angelica's cheeks reddened. "Dammit, Cade—"

"Does that dress button?"

"What?"

He yanked a black wool dress from its hanger. "Does it button?" he said impatiently. "You know, do you get into it by just slipping your arms into it."

"Well, yes, but—"

She gasped as he tugged the blanket from her. "Here," he said crisply, and held out the dress. "Put this on."

She wanted to say no, to tell him what he could do with the dress—but that would have only left her standing before him in her underwear. She hissed a word at him that made him laugh while he helped her into the dress, but she slapped his hand away and fumbled the buttons closed on her own.

Barefoot, her hair streaming down her back, she confronted him.

"All right," she said. "What's going on here?"

"I've just faced facts, that's all. I've realized that—unfortunately for us both—I'm dependent on your assistance."

"Well, that must be painful to admit!"

"I've also realized that, left to your own devices, you'll probably bring your house down around your ears."

"That's ridiculous."

"And then there's the problem of me sitting around, tapping my toes while I wait for you to get yourself to the office."

"Why don't you just tell me the bottom line, Cade?"

"I'd rather start at the top," he said with a little smile. "The first item on the agenda is breakfast. Bacon, eggs, a gallon of coffee—and a handful of aspirin." He plucked a pair of shoes from the bottom of the wardrobe and put them at her feet. "Can you get those on without help?"

"Don't talk to me as if I were four years old," Angelica snapped as she slipped her feet into the shoes. "I understand now. You're so worried about me making it to the office that you're going to take me there yourself." Her smile was edged with frost. "How generous."

"I'd hardly expect you to go to work today."

"Then why—"

"Today, you'll just take it easy." He took her arm. She stiffened and tried to wrench free, but his fingers clamped down on her wrist. "We'll go to my hotel, check you into my suite—"

"Are you crazy?"

"You can nap the afternoon away while I catch up on paperwork."

"You *are* crazy," she sputtered. "I'd never—"

"It's a big suite, Angelica. Did I mention that? Two bedrooms, two bathrooms—"

"It could be the size of Buckingham Palace and I wouldn't share it with you!"

Cade's smile vanished. "Perhaps you've forgotten that you work for Landon Enterprises."

"That doesn't give you the right to order me to move into your hotel room!"

"I just explained that you'll have your own room and your own bath."

"I don't care! I'm not going to do it!"

"That's your prerogative—in which case, I'll do what's best for Gordon Oil."

The way he said it made her heart skip a beat. "Meaning?"

"Meaning, you'll stay away from the office until that hand is completely healed. I'll continue you on salary, of course."

"Dammit, Cade, what's the rest? I can hear that brain of yours clicking, I *know* you've got something else in mind."

"Well, since you'll be incapacitated and since Gordon Oil can't operate itself, I'll have to put someone in charge."

"What?"

"You heard me." His voice hardened. "I'll need someone responsible at Gordon's, and it wouldn't be logical or even possible to hire the proper individual on a temporary basis. I'm afraid I'll have to let you go."

"No! The verbal contract—"

"Assuming there is one, it would be rendered null and void by your inability to fulfill your role as director." The lie was so logical, and fell from his lips with such authority, that it might as well have come from a lawyer, he thought proudly.

"But," she said, "but..."

But if Cade forced her out of the company, what chance would she have of getting back in?

She stared at the handsome face, the polite smile, the dark blue eyes that mocked her.

"Why are you doing this to me?" she whispered.

"I'm not doing anything to you, Angelica, I'm simply protecting Landon's investment. I'm suggesting a practical offer of assistance. If you choose to refuse it..."

He shrugged and smiled politely. Angelica fought for control, knowing that to slap that arrogant smile from his face would only be self-defeating. When she finally spoke, her voice trembled with anger.

"You're not contemptible, Cade," she said, "you're despicable."

She pulled away from him and made her way to the stairs. Cade let her go, watching her as she made her way down them, his face like stone. He didn't realize he'd been holding his breath until she reached the front door. Then he exhaled sharply and loped down the steps after her.

CHAPTER EIGHT

His suite, Cade had said, was spacious.

One look told Angelica that "spacious" was far too simple a word to describe his accommodations.

He unlocked the door, and she stepped past him into a sitting room that seemed to stretch interminably to meet a curtained wall of glass.

The room was beautiful. The furniture was spare and elegant, depending on pale woods, paler leathers and linear design for impact. Paintings in vivid primary colors brightened the soft white walls; the white marble floor was bare, except for one extraordinarily beautiful handwoven rya rug.

Cade shut the door behind him, dropped the keys into a terra-cotta bowl and turned to her.

"My bedroom is the one to the right," he said. "Yours is through that door on the left." He smiled tightly. "They're the same, except for the views. If you prefer mine, say so. We can swap."

Change rooms? Sleep in the room that was Cade's? In his bed? For some inexplicable reason, the thought made her breathless, but she only smiled coolly.

"Such gallantry, Cade. Who'd have expected it?"

"Not you," he said with a little laugh, "we both know that." He walked to the windows and drew open the curtains. "Tomorrow, when you're feeling better—"

"I feel perfectly fine."

"Tomorrow," he repeated, "we'll see about getting you something to wear."

"What does that mean? I have plenty of things to wear. If you'd given me time to pack—"

"Right." He smiled coolly as he turned toward her. "You've got enough suits to stock a department store, but nothing—"

But nothing soft that would cling to her soft curves, that would be the right color to bring out the emerald of her eyes or the fire in her hair.

Damn! Where had that bit of nonsense come from? Cade scowled and put his hands on his hips.

"I thought I made myself clear. I've no intention of standing around like a fool, waiting for you to try to get yourself ready for work in the mornings."

"And I've no intention of wasting money on frivolous things I don't need!"

"You don't have to. I'll pay for whatever you need."

"That's out of the question. I am not going to permit you to—"

"Dammit," he snapped, "get down off that high horse! You were injured on the job, remember? If proper clothing is necessary for your rehabilitation, your employer is obligated to pay all necessary expenses—and Landon's is your employer, isn't it?"

God, he thought, he sounded like a fool. What in hell was the matter with him?

"Look," he said, "I'll check with my legal people, if that will make you feel better." And brother Grant would agree, Cade thought, he'd see to that. He sank down into one of a pair of low, white leather couches that flanked a teakwood coffee table, linked his hands behind his head and sighed wearily. "In the meantime, spare me the speeches. I'm not up to a feminist lecture just now."

"Anything I say that you don't agree with is not a—"

"Let's try a neutral subject. What do you think of your new accommodations? Do they satisfy you?"

"My own home satisfied me."

"It's a simple question, Angelica." He sat up and glared at her. "Will you be comfortable here?"

"Why? Does my comfort—or my opinion—matter?" She shrugged her shoulders. "If you're waiting for me to ooh and ah, forget it. You've gotten your way. I'm here, and now I'll just have to make the best of things."

Cade opened his mouth, started to answer, and then he sighed, leaned his head back again and shut his eyes.

"You know something, sugar? I'm too tired to argue."

Angelica's gaze swept over him. Cade Landon, too weary to argue? It hardly seemed possible—but he did look tired, she thought suddenly. The trip from Dallas to Notrees and back meant he'd flown eight hundred miles. He'd stayed at her side all through her ordeal with the scorpion, and topped things off by spending the night in a chair that wouldn't have been comfortable for a man half his size.

She felt a twinge of guilt. In his own way, he'd tried to be kind to her. It wasn't his fault that he thought kindness meant taking over a person's life.

"Cade?" Angelica cleared her throat. "I suppose—I suppose I should thank you for all you've done."

"You already did. You choked out a thank-you that almost sounded like you meant it a couple of hours ago, remember?" He opened one eye and looked at her. "Do it again and I'm liable to figure that scorpion sting's affected your sanity."

Her lips compressed, but after a minute she saw his lips twitch. She smiled.

"Actually," she said. "I'm feeling much better."

Cade sat up and looked at her. "I'm glad to hear it. How about if I send down for some lunch?"

Angelica shuddered. "After the breakfast we just ate? No, no lunch for me."

"Tea, then? Or coffee?"

"No, really, I don't want anything—except a bath."

"Of course." He rose to his feet and walked slowly to where she stood. "Tell you what. You go on to your room and take a nap."

She smiled at him. "I will—after I bathe."

He smiled back at her. "Maybe later."

"Maybe later?" Her brows lifted and she gave a little laugh. "What do you mean, maybe later? I don't recall asking permission."

"Look, you've been feeling pretty woozy." Cade put his arm around her shoulders and walked her slowly toward her door. "I don't want you to push things."

"I'm not going to push anything. I *was* woozy, but I'm fine now. A bath's just what I need."

"Not just yet."

Angelica swung toward him. "What is this, Cade?" Her smile was stiff at the edges. "Has the city gone on water rationing without my knowing?"

He chuckled. "Not to worry, sugar. There's plenty of water, enough to fill the Jacuzzi in your bathroom and mine a million times over."

"Well, that's good news," she said lightly. "For a minute there, I thought—"

"I don't want you to bathe until we're sure you won't feel light-headed again. Passing out in a tub full of water—or in the shower, for that matter—could be dangerous."

"I appreciate your concern," Angelica said politely. "And I'll think about it, but—"

"There's not anything to think about," Cade said with a little smile. "You know I'm right."

"Listen here, Cade—"

"You can bathe when we decide you're up to it."

"We?" she said, *"we?"* She tossed the hair from her face. "I know you like to think you're emperor of the universe, but you're beginning to take your paranoia a bit far."

"Look, I know you're tired and irritable—"

"I am neither tired nor irritable! I am just not interested in continuing a stupid discussion about if and when I should take a bath!"

"Well, we don't have to decide now." He was still smiling, but it was the kind of smile people reserved for incompetents and children. "Take your nap first. We can discuss it again after you wake up." He touched the tip of his finger to her lips, then turned her around and propelled her gently through the doorway and into her room. "Sleep well. Remember, if you need me—"

"Don't hold your breath!"

Angelica kicked back her heel and slammed the door shut.

She stood still for a moment, struggling for control, and then she clapped her hand to her forehead.

Arrogant? Insolent? The word to describe Cade Landon hadn't been invented yet. The more time they spent together, the worse he got.

And she was tired of it.

He was going to decide when she might shower?

"Ha!" she said into the silence.

She'd take a dozen baths, and another dozen showers, if that was what she wanted.

She kicked off her shoes, undid the buttons on her dress and stepped out of it. It was just a miracle Cade hadn't insisted on undressing her again. Not that she'd have let him. Last night had been different; she'd been sick and groggy and almost out on her feet, which was why he'd been able to boss her around...

...which was why she'd behaved the way she had when he'd put her to bed. Heat flooded her skin as she remembered what had happened, that dizzying kiss, the touch of his hands on her breasts...

She shook her head impatiently as she padded across the plush carpet. Who was Cade Landon, to think he could give her orders?

The bathroom was a revelation. It was enormous, as big as her living room at home, and it gleamed with marble, gold plating and mirrors. A small TV hung from a corner bracket. With a little smile, she switched it on. Men in Arab dress dashed across the screen on the backs of high-stepping horses, and the familiar theme music from *Lawrence of Arabia* filled the room.

Humming happily, Angelica turned her attention to the room's fixtures. The shower was grand, a big glass enclosure with spray heads everywhere.

Ah, but the tub was something else entirely. It was a sunken oval of shiny black that looked as if it could accommodate a family of four without crowding—and it had a hand-spray attachment. She could wash her hair, rinse it, then sit in the water until her toes began to shrivel.

She smiled as she turned on the taps. A long, luxurious soak would go a long way toward making her feel more human.

Still humming, she plucked tiny packets of scented bubble bath and shampoo from a small wicker basket on the vanity. Her injured hand hampered her a little, but eventually she managed to tear open the bubble bath and pour it into the rapidly filling tub.

Angelica shut off the water, stepped carefully down into the tub and sighed with pleasure. She bathed quickly, washed her hair despite the occasional twinges of pain in her hand, and then, at last, she lay back and closed her eyes.

It was heaven, letting the bubble-filled water lap gently over her breasts while the music streamed down over her like a waterfall of sound . . .

"Angelica!"

Her eyes flew open. Cade was standing in the bathroom doorway. With a cry of outrage, she sank lower into the bubbles.

"What do you think you're doing?" she shrieked. "You get the hell out of this bathroom!"

"What are you doing in that tub?"

"What does it look like I'm doing? Damn you, Cade, get out!"

"The hell I will!" He folded his arms over his chest, his face stony. "You were supposed to be napping."

"Do you have difficulty understanding English? Get out of this room!"

"But *were* you napping?" he continued nastily. "No, you were not!"

"And how did you find that out?" Angelica demanded. "By sneaking into my room!"

"I thought to look in and see how you were doing."

"Ha!"

"I knocked, but you didn't answer. So I opened your door—"

"And you decided to come barging into my bathroom!"

"I heard noise coming from the bathroom," he said coldly, "and even though I knocked again—" He reached up and punched the button on the TV set. A tense silence filled the room. "Dammit, Angelica, for all I knew you'd fallen and broken your fool neck!"

"The only neck that's going to be broken is yours, if you don't turn around and get out of here!"

"What in hell's wrong with you?" A look of thunderous disapproval spread across his face. "Weren't you paying attention when we discussed this?"

"Are you deaf, Cade?" She pointed her hand at the door. "Go away!"

"You said you'd call me if you needed me," he growled as he started toward her. "You said—"

"I said no such thing." She slid lower in the concealing bubbles. "No one says much when you're around. You do all the talking."

"You could have gotten dizzy. You could have fallen. Knowing your track record, you could have drowned! Hell, this morning you were determined to burn down your house."

"I was not. Besides, I was ill then. I'm fine now, and..." She took a ragged breath, then spat out a word never used by anyone at Miss Palmer's Academy. "What am I doing, explaining myself to you? If you don't get out of here this instant, I'm going to scream."

"So scream," he said coldly, and snatched a bath towel from the heated rack. "See if I give a damn. See if anybody gives a damn! Go on, scream and let the staff and the guests come running. Let them crowd in here and then maybe you can tell all of us why you're so pigheaded.''

''I don't have to explain anything to anybody, Cade Landon! I am my own person.''

''You mean, you're your own worst enemy. Come on, woman. Get out of that tub.''

''Get out of this bathroom!''

Cade's eyes narrowed to slits. ''You've got five seconds to get moving.''

''I'm not going anywhere, not until you're on the other side of that door.''

''Five seconds, or I'll come in and get you.''

She stared at him, enraged.

''One,'' he said.

Would he do it? No. Not even Cade Landon was that crazy.

''Two.''

For one thing, he was fully dressed.

''Three.''

For another, he had to know that she would sooner drown than let him drag her from the tub.

''Four.''

On the other hand, this was the man who'd spent the night in her bedroom, who'd all but blackmailed her into moving into this hotel...

''Five. That's it, sugar. Here I come.''

''Damn you, Cade!'' Angelica touched the tip of her tongue to her lips. ''You cannot really expect me to— to get out of this tub and into that towel while you hold it.''

''Can't I?'' His lips drew back from his teeth. ''It's bad enough I'm going to have to pick up yesterday's hospital bill, but if you expect me to pay the fees when you step out of that tub, slip and break your silly neck, you'd better think again.''

"What I think," Angelica said, her voice trembling, "is that it's always best to placate a madman!" She looked at the towel in his hands. Stretched to its limits, it was almost the size of a blanket. "Lift that towel higher. And if you so much as touch me, I'll scratch out your eyes."

"There's nothing to worry about," he snapped. "I prefer my women with at least a modicum of femininity."

He lifted the towel. She took a breath, rose and stepped quickly from the tub. With one deft movement, she stepped into the towel, snatched it from him, wrapped it around herself and knotted it above her breasts.

"I am out of the tub," she said. "Now you get out of this bathroom. And out of my bedroom. I am going to dry off, get dressed, go home and lock my door. Tomorrow, I will be at the office at whatever hour you like. And I will stay there until whatever hour you like." Her chin shot forward. "And if you harass me or threaten me or do any of the impossible things you've done in the last twenty-four hours, so help me, I'll—I'll bring charges against you!"

He didn't move.

"I don't understand you," he said, shaking his head. "Is it beyond you to accept help when you need it?"

"Help? Is that what you call your—your interference? You don't offer help, Cade. You control, you command, you try to take over another person's life!"

Cade's mouth narrowed. "I do not."

"You do. It's the truth, but you don't give a damn about the truth!" She glared at him. "You don't give a damn about anything I say, because I'm a woman! If I were a man—"

Cade grabbed her by the shoulders. "If you were a man, I wouldn't be in this mess! I'd have driven you home last night, poured you a shot of whiskey and said listen, pal, hire yourself a housekeeper and send the bill to me."

"Well? Why didn't you?" Angelica lifted her chin in defiance. "What does my sex have to do with anything?"

The question jolted him with its directness. What *did* it have to do with anything? She was a woman, yes, a gorgeous woman—but she wasn't the type that appealed to him. She was a copper-curled spitfire and nothing would ever matter half as much to her as her own ambition.

His hands tightened on her, and suddenly he knew the answer.

Angelica Gordon was nothing he wanted—and everything he had to have. Hell, he'd known it all the time, but he'd refused to admit it.

There would be no peace for him until he took Angelica Gordon to bed and subdued her in the oldest way a man could subdue a woman.

Then she'd be out of his system, and for good.

Something of what he was thinking must have showed in his face. He could tell by the sudden intake of her breath, by the way a pulse leaped to nervous life in the hollow of her throat.

"Cade," she said, "Cade, I'm warning you—"

Hell, it was what they needed from each other, what all the pettiness and snarling was about. It was about being oil and water, yin and yang, fire and ice, it was nothing but a hot, physical need that had been eating at them both from the beginning.

And there was only one way to put an end to it.

"Cade," Angelica said again, and he smiled.

"What?" he said. His voice sounded thick; his tongue felt thick, as if he were drunk. And he was. He was drunk on the remembered taste of that rosebud mouth, that creamy skin. "What are you warning me about, sugar?"

"I'm—I'm warning you not to—not to..."

She caught her breath as his hands moved against her skin. His fingers were callused and rough; the sensations they drew from her nerve endings sent a race of flame along her flesh.

"Cade," she said.

"Yes." He backed her against the vanity, his hands cupping her shoulders. His voice was rough, with the texture of wild honey. "I'm here, sugar. I'm right here."

She made a little sound as he bent and touched his mouth to her throat. Oh, God. What was happening to her? Her bones were turning to liquid; her skin was flooding with heat.

His teeth nipped at the tender curve of her shoulder. She whimpered softly, and her hands came up and lay against his chest.

"Cade," she said shakily, "Cade..."

Was that all she was capable of saying? Just his name, over and over? She caught her breath as his hands slid down her body, then slipped to the front of the towel where the knotted edges overlapped.

"I need to touch you," he said, and she gasped as he put his hands under the towel and curved them against her thighs.

"Oh," she whispered, "oh..."

Cade kissed her mouth, his lips sucking and biting hers.

"Do you want me to stop?" he said thickly.

Her gaze flew to his. His eyes were dark, so dark she felt as if she might drown and be lost in them.

"Angelica?" His hands rose, cupped her naked buttocks. "Shall I stop?"

She gave a little groan as she leaned into him. Her arm snaked around his neck; she lifted herself to him and put her open mouth against his.

She clung to him as he carried her into the bedroom, his lips hot against hers. He put her on the bed, then came down beside her, still holding her, still kissing her and devouring the sweet nectar of her mouth.

His hand moved over her, over the towel, following the curve of her breast, the sweet indentation of her waist, the rounding of her hip.

"Cade," she whispered.

His eyes went to her face. She was watching him, her eyes wide and expectant. Her face was flushed, her mouth already soft and swollen by his, and he wondered, with one last, brief flash of sanity, if he would be able to keep from thrusting into her before he'd even explored the wonders of her body.

"Angelica." He swallowed hard, took a deep breath. "I—I need you," he whispered. "I want you so badly..."

With a groan, he fumbled at the knot that kept the towel together. His fingers felt numb and clumsy. They trembled with the nervousness of a schoolboy. And it was hard to draw breath into his lungs as he slowly spread the edges of the towel apart.

Everything that was happening might have been happening for the first time.

The breath sighed from his lungs as he looked at her. She was so beautiful. Her breasts were sweetly rounded, her nipples as pink and delicate as the petals of a rose. He lowered his head, kissing first one swollen tip and then the other, and her cries of pleasure were almost his undoing.

His hand slid to her waist, which was slender, then to her hips, which had surely been meant to fit the curve of his hands. Her belly was silken, her navel small and delicate. He longed to touch his tongue to it and taste its sweetness, but first, God, first he had to touch those copper curls that framed her femininity, he had to move his hand over that softness and into what lay beyond.

Angelica cried out as his fingers slid against her damp heat. She arched toward him, her hands clutching at his shoulders, her body trembling with desire.

Could she have dreamed it would be like this? The touch of his hands, the feel of his mouth, the scent of proud, conquering male. She was turning to flame in his arms, desperate for his final possession.

Possession? But how could she want that? It was a word she hated, a concept she abhorred.

"Angel," Cade whispered, "my sweet Angel."

He kissed her again, slowly and deeply, his tongue moving in her mouth as his fingers moved against her swollen flesh. She was panting now, she could feel her sweat mingling with his. She was a swirling, dizzying mix of emotions, need and desire and passion all mixed in with something more, something that transcended desire. She wanted to touch him, to be touched, but she wanted more, she wanted—she wanted...

He kissed her, and her thoughts broke into a thousand separate pieces.

"Yes," she said against his mouth, "yes, please."

Cade looked into her face. Her eyes were dark, the pupils so huge that her irises were visible only as a circular hint of emerald. She was writhing beneath him, begging him for release, but she was no more desperate than he. His muscles were so taut that he was trembling, but he would not hurry this moment. He wanted to pleasure her forever, touch her forever.

But then she moved, shifting her hips, and he knew he could wait no longer.

She watched through half-lowered lashes as he pulled off his clothing. Surely, her heart would break with the masculine beauty of him. Her gaze swept over the powerful shoulders and arms, the muscled chest, the narrow waist and hips that tapered into long, muscular legs. His shaft arrowed from its nest of soft dark curls, strong, unashamedly male, and incredibly exciting.

Angelica hesitated, then reached out and touched him.

Cade groaned and caught her hand in his.

"Don't," he said. "If you do..." He kissed her and moved between her thighs. "Angel," he whispered, and when her eyes were hot on his, he lifted her to him and entered her with slow, sweet deliberation, savoring her tightness and her heat as her body welcomed his.

She cried out his name, and he began to move inside her, long, deep strokes that took her to the brink of release but never quite let her tumble over the edge. She could feel the cost of that taut control in his muscles as she clasped his shoulders, in the slick dampness that glazed his skin.

"Now," she sobbed, "Cade, now, please..."

She arched off the bed as she cried out. Cade threw back his head and exploded within her, and Angelica felt herself shatter into thousands of bright, crystalline shards.

CHAPTER NINE

CADE rolled to his side, still holding Angelica tightly in the curve of his arm.

He could feel the muscles in his body slackening, letting go the last vestiges of the almost painfully elemental compulsion that had hammered him toward those last, frenzied moments of release. His racing heart began to slow; he became aware of the coolness of the air on his sweat-slicked skin, the slight abrasiveness of the blanket tangled beneath him...

...the softness and the sweetness of the woman lying in his arms.

He rose up on his elbow and gazed at her with wonder and admiration.

"Angel?" he whispered, but she didn't answer. He smiled to himself. She had fallen asleep, and in his arms.

It was silly, but the realization made him feel special.

How beautiful she was. Her hair streamed across his pillow like ribbons of copper; her dark lashes were silken against her cheeks. Her mouth was reddened and softly swollen from his kisses, her face and breasts still bore the flush of passion.

And now she was his. Cade's jaw tightened. Yes. She was his, he had branded her with his desire, and she would never, could never belong to any other man...

What the hell was the matter with him?

He slipped his arm from beneath her shoulders. She sighed and rolled away from him, but she didn't waken. Carefully, he pushed the blankets aside, got to his feet and made his way to the bathroom. He stepped into the shower and turned on the water, letting it beat down full force and hot on his shoulders.

He wasn't a man given to sentimentality, not even in the soft afterglow of sex, not even when the sex had been terrific—and he had to admit, this had been. Angelica had been so tight, she'd been so wild yet so innocent in his arms—for a moment, he'd almost thought she'd never been with a man before. And he'd almost wished—he'd wished...

"Dammit!" Cade shut off the water. He was being stupid. OK. The sex they'd shared had been great, better than any he'd ever known.

But sex was all it was. After a while, it would run its course.

It always did.

Angelica heard the shower running and let out a sigh of relief.

She hadn't been certain that she could fool Cade into thinking she was asleep, and if he'd tried to take her in his arms again, if he'd said one sweet, tender word...

She sighed and closed her eyes.

Who would have dreamed that making love was like this?

Until moments ago, she'd been a virgin. She knew that was almost laughable in today's world, but to want to make love with a man you had to let yourself feel something. You had to want to share everything you were, everything you could be—and she had never felt that, never even understood it.

Why would any woman want to feel so exposed and vulnerable?

Now she knew that the reality was even worse. She felt more than exposed, more than vulnerable.

She felt terrified.

Part of her wanted to stay right here, waiting for Cade to come back to bed, take her in his arms and make love to her again.

And part of her wanted to get up and run for her life.

How could something so wonderful have left her feeling so confused? Minutes ago, she'd lain in Cade's arms and burned at his touch. She'd shattered into a million pieces, yet become more than whole. But once the fires had dwindled and she'd drifted safely back to the tranquility of his embrace, she'd felt something else.

She'd felt secure and protected, as if he had given her not just his passion but his strength.

And that was nothing but insanity.

Wasn't it?

How could there be security and protection when men made the rules?

Men didn't shelter or protect, they smothered.

Just look how Cade had smothered her in the past twenty-four hours, turning her from an independent woman into—into...

She sat up and tunneled her fingers through her hair. How could she have let herself get so sloppily sentimental? Just because Cade was a good lover was no reason for her to become rhapsodic.

And he had been a good lover, she thought with a little tremor, a wonderful lover, fierce but tender, as giving as he was demanding.

Why wouldn't he be? Women probably threw themselves at his feet. He'd have had hundreds of chances to refine his technique by now, thousands of opportunities to learn the special places a woman wanted to be touched and kissed...

Pain choked her heart. Everything he'd done to her, he had done before. Worse, he would do all those things again to the women who would follow her, all those wondrous, secret things he'd taught her, those fantastic moments they'd shared.

She flung back the blankets, shot to her feet and snatched up her clothing. Enough was enough! That damned medicine must have wrecked her thought processes, destroyed them so completely that she didn't know when it was time to cut her losses and run.

Cut and run. If that wasn't basic psychological philosophy, it certainly ought to be—

She gasped as Cade's hands fell on her shoulders.

"Hey," he said, and turned her toward him. A towel was knotted around his waist; drops of water glistened in his hair and on his shoulders. A puzzled smile tilted across his mouth. "Where are you going, sugar?"

Angelica took a deep breath. There was no sense in beating around the bush.

"I'm leaving."

His smile grew even more puzzled. "I don't understand. What do you mean, you're leaving?"

"Come on, Cade." She shrugged his hands away and reached for her dress. "It's not a difficult concept." Quickly, she slipped the dress on and began buttoning it closed. "I am going home." Her eyes met his and she smiled as coolly as she could. "Is that clear enough for you?"

He wasn't smiling now, she saw with satisfaction; he was looking like a little boy who'd been caught with his hand in the cookie jar.

If only he'd put on some clothes!

"Don't be a fool, Angelica. You know you're not going anywhere."

"But I am." She tossed the hair from her face and combed her fingers through it. "And before you bother telling me you'll remove me from my job if I don't perform my duties adequately—"

"To hell with your job!" His hand closed around her wrist and he pulled her toward him. "I'm talking about us."

"Us? What do you mean, us?" Angelica's mouth narrowed. "There is no us, Cade."

"No?" He jerked his head toward the bed behind her. "Are you going to tell me I imagined what went on in that bed this afternoon?"

She flushed, but her eyes remained fixed on his. "That was—it was just something that happened."

Cade's lips drew back from his teeth. "Really," he said softly.

"And it's certainly not going to happen again!"

He laughed softly. "Is that a warning, sugar, or a challenge?"

"It's a statement of fact. Just because you managed to—to seduce me doesn't mean—"

"Ah. I see. This piece needs a villain, and I'm it."

"Look, Cade, I don't want to quarrel about this. I just—"

"You just think you're going to turn around, walk away from me, and that I'm going to let you?"

"*Let* me?" Angelica smiled tightly. "You can't stop me."

His smile was slow and sexy, and it sent a flash of heat sizzling through her bones.

"Can't I?"

"Dammit, Cade—"

"Dammit, Angelica," he said, his voice soft and teasing, and he cupped her face in his hands and kissed her.

She let him, sensing that to fight him would only give him the advantage—and he already had that, she thought helplessly, as she felt his mouth settle gently over hers. The cool touch of his lips made her want to stroke the tip of her tongue against his, to put her hands against his naked chest and give herself up to the kiss.

She swayed a little when he drew back, but she met his gaze without flinching.

"Nice," she said. "Very nice—but it doesn't change anything. I'm still leaving."

Cade's face turned to stone. "The hell you are!"

"Cade, don't do this! You can't force me to—"

She cried out as his hands went to her shoulders and he spun her around.

"Look at yourself in the mirror," he growled. "Take a good, long look, sugar, and tell me what you see."

"This is preposterous. What do you want? A testimonial? You're a good lover, you know it, and I—"

Her breath caught as she stared at her reflection. She had never seen herself like this before. Her mouth was still soft and swollen from Cade's kisses, her throat bore the faint impression of his teeth—but it was much more than that which held her enthralled.

Her eyes had never been so deep and dark a green, her skin so luminous. There was a glow about her, a look that said she was a woman who had been loved, and loved well.

Her eyes met Cade's. "Are you really going to walk away from the man who made you look like that?" he said softly.

Angelica choked out a laugh. "My God, listen to yourself! Are you really going to take credit for—for…"

"For what happened in that bed?" He shook his head, his eyes still locked on the mirrored image of hers. "No, Angel," he whispered, cupping her shoulders. "If I'm the man who's made you look the way you do, then you're the woman who's made me feel—made me feel…"

A muscle knotted in his jaw. What did he feel? He wasn't sure any more. A little while ago, he'd told himself that what he'd shared with this woman was nothing but fantastic sex.

Now, looking into the emerald-green reflection of her eyes, he wasn't so sure.

All he knew for certain was that something was happening here, and he'd be a fool to let either of them walk away from it until they knew what it was.

Slowly, he turned Angelica toward him.

"I don't know," he said softly. "I only know that we were tremendous together." He lifted his hand and ran his fingers through her hair. "You were the sun, all flame and fire scorching my flesh when you took me inside you, and I—I was a god, fated to be consumed and reborn by flame."

Angelica shuddered. "Cade," she whispered, "please, don't do this. It isn't—it isn't fair. I admit, what we did was—"

"We made love, Angel. Is that so hard to accept?"

She swallowed dryly, trying to ignore the feel of his hand as it moved against her cheek.

"We—we slept together," she said shakily. "And—and I admit, it was—it was—"

"Fantastic," he said, his mouth against her throat.

"Yes." Her head fell back as his lips traced a soft line of kisses down her skin. "Yes," she sighed. "But—but—"

"Angelica."

His fingers were at the buttons of her dress, opening them one by one. Stop him, she told herself—but she knew, in her heart, that she didn't want to stop him. Not now, not ever.

The dress fell away from her, and the rest of her clothes. Cade's eyes darkened as he looked at her.

"Angel," he said in a husky whisper, "my perfect Angel."

His hands rose and cupped her breasts; she moaned as she watched his thumbs move across the pale pink crests.

"Do you still want to leave me?" he whispered.

Her eyes met his, and her blood, already pulsing through her veins, began to pound. Something was happening, she could feel it deep inside her. She had never needed anyone in her life, but she needed Cade, needed him not just to bury himself inside her but—but...

"Tell me you won't leave me," he said in a rough whisper.

The words burst from her lips. "I won't leave you!" Angelica's voice broke as she went into his arms. "Never," she said fiercely, "never!"

And, as Cade bore her down into the soft tangle of sheets and blankets, she finally faced the truth.

She had built her life in rejection of everything Cade Landon represented.

But that hadn't kept her from falling desperately, hopelessly in love with him.

They ate dinner by candlelight at a small table beside the window, sipping Kristal champagne and dining on lobster bisque and *boeuf en croute*.

The china was exquisite, the crystal perfect—and so, Cade insisted, was their dress.

He wore the bottom half of a pair of blue cotton pajamas.

Angelica wore the top.

"Don't look at me like that," she said, with a little laugh.

"Look at you how?" he said, and grinned.

"You know how."

Cade reached across the little table and tugged gently at a long, coppery curl that lay against her shoulder.

"You look like a little girl," he said softly.

She smiled. "I'm twenty-seven," she said. "That's hardly a little girl."

"I'll bet you were the prettiest little girl in all of Texas."

Angelica made a face. "Not me. I hated the color of my hair, hated my freckles—"

"So you moved East and became the prettiest little girl there," Cade said, and smiled.

Angelica laughed. "You mean, I became the girl with the red hair, the freckles and the funny accent."

"Does your mother still live back East?"

"No. She died when I was in my last year of college."

Cade looked at her. "What about brothers? Or sisters?"

"There's just me." She smiled wistfully. "It must be nice, having a big family."

He shrugged. "Well, it has its moments."

Angelica propped her chin in her hand. "OK," she said, "it's your turn. Tell me about Cade Landon."

He grinned. "You already know most of it. I'm handsome, intelligent..."

"And modest." She reached forward and touched her fingertip to his slightly crooked nose. "How'd that happen?"

Cade laughed. "I wish I could tell you something romantic, that I broke it in some waterfront dive in Singapore or something, but the truth is that I got it busted years ago, in a fight on an oil rig."

"A fight?"

"Yeah. Some bozo decided I looked too green to be giving orders, that the only authority I had came from the Landon name."

"And you decided to show him otherwise."

"I never got anything from the Landon name," Cade said with a tight smile. "Except maybe the desire to disassociate myself from the man who'd passed it along to me."

"You and your father didn't get along?" Angelica said softly.

Cade laughed. "The understatement of the century, Angel. He was good at giving orders—"

"And you were good at ignoring them?"

He shrugged his shoulders. "Let's just say I didn't like having somebody make the rules for the way I was supposed to live my life."

"No." Angelica looked at him. "Nobody likes that."

"Uh-oh," he said softly. "That's an ominous tone the lady has. Is that what you think, that I've been trying to make rules for you to live by?"

She smiled. "Well..."

"Angel, that's not fair. You've been sick. I just—" He smiled. "OK. Maybe I did take over a little, but—"

"But?"

He reached across the table and slowly slipped his hand inside the pajama top.

"But from now on," he said, his eyes turning to smoke, "I'll only take over where it counts."

Seconds later, they were locked in each other's arms.

The next morning, Cade sat in a chair opposite the bed. He was dressed in a dark blue suit, a white shirt and a striped tie, and he was sipping a cup of coffee.

But mostly, he was watching Angelica as she slept and thinking that the word "beautiful" didn't really do her justice.

Getting up an hour ago and leaving her warm, sweetly scented body had been difficult, but there was an important business matter that left him no choice—and before he left, he'd had something important to do.

He thought of the gaily wrapped boxes waiting in the sitting room. He could hardly wait to see her face when she opened them and saw the things he'd bought her, the silky camisoles and teddies, the soft cashmere dress that was the same green as her eyes.

She was too beautiful to hide behind tweeds and dark wools, and she didn't have to, not anymore. Cade smiled to himself as he sipped his coffee. He had learned a lot about her in the past twenty-four hours, enough to understand why she'd been so determined to prove herself at Gordon Oil.

It wasn't ambition that drove her. It was pain.

He could almost see her, the little girl with the red hair, at home neither in Texas nor back East, losing first her home and her father, and then her mother.

But now she had him. And he would protect her, and love her, forever.

He knew that now, knew that he'd been kidding himself, trying to pretend she was just another woman.

She wasn't. She was his.

"Cade?"

He looked up, and he felt a smile curve across his mouth. Angelica was blinking the sleep from her eyes, staring at him across a tangle of blankets, and it was all he could do to keep from hurrying across the room and taking her in his arms.

"Good morning, sugar. Did you sleep well?"

She sat up against the pillows, clutching the blanket to her chin.

"What time is it?" she said. Her gaze swept over him and she frowned. "Have I overslept? Cade, you should have—"

"Easy, Angel." He rose, walked to the bed, sat down next to her and took her in his arms. "Aren't you going to kiss me good morning?"

He kissed her slowly and deeply, determinedly ignoring the swift quickening of his body as her mouth opened to his. Finally, she leaned back in his arms and smiled.

"You should have woken me," she whispered, smiling into his eyes. "Now you'll have to wait while I get ready for work, too."

"No work today," he said lightly.

Angelica's brow furrowed. "But—"

"Well, a little work, maybe." He rose from the bed and stepped into the sitting room. When he came back, his arms were loaded with packages. "You've got to try on all this stuff and tell me if you like my choices."

She looked at him blankly. "What is all this?"

Cade dumped the boxes on the bed. "Open one and find out."

He handed her a small box. She smiled hesitantly, undid the paper—and withdrew a camisole and panties of pale pink silk.

She looked at him, her expression halfway between a smile and a frown.

"Cade, I can't accept this. I told you—"

"Wrong size?"

"No. But—"

"Wrong color?"

"The color's perfect, but—"

"See what you think of this."

"This" proved to be a dress of forest-green cashmere. It was incredibly beautiful—and, Angelica knew, incredibly expensive.

"Cade," she said sternly, "I cannot—"

"We agreed, you can't wear the clothing you have at home until your hand is better."

"It *is* better. Much. And we didn't agree. You announced that—"

"I'm not taking over, or making the rules, or whatever it is you thought I did last night."

Angelica sighed. "You're not?"

"Hell, no. I'm just giving my woman a gift." He bent down, tilted her face to his and kissed her. "There's no law against that, is there?"

His woman, she thought, his woman...

The words were so simple. But their effect wasn't simple at all. Part of her thrilled to them—and part recoiled.

"Sugar?" Cade stroked the curls from her cheeks. "If we really have to argue about this, we'll have to do it later. Right now, I've got about half an hour to get clear across town."

"But I thought—aren't we going to work today?"

We, he thought, and he smiled.

"No, sugar, we're not. Well, you're not, anyway. But I've got a meeting with Jim Larrabee. I phoned him and tried to cancel, but—"

"Jim Larrabee?"

"From that company that sold you some drilling equipment a few weeks ago, remember? I want to talk to him about a new schedule of payments."

Payments, Angelica thought, and schedules. How quickly she'd forgotten all about business—and all about Gordon Oil.

"I know who he is, Cade. And I tried to get him to agree to a new schedule, but—"

"He'll agree to this."

She felt herself bristling at the smug self-assurance in his tone.

"How nice to be so confident. What kind of schedule is it?"

"There's no point in my boring you with the details, sugar. Tell you what—you pick a restaurant for lunch. Do you like Tex-Mex food? I know this little place for ribs that—"

Angelica's mouth firmed. "You can hardly bore me with the details of a deal that affects my company," she said stiffly.

"Come on, Angel. Isn't it time we gave that up?"

"Gave what up?" Her voice hardened. "I'm still in charge of Gordon's, Cade, in case you'd forgotten."

"No," he said carefully, "no, I hadn't forgotten. But—"

But what? Every instinct told him this wasn't the time for a confrontation. Cade blew out his breath.

"Just what I said, Angel. I didn't want to bore you with the details." He smiled. "Not this morning."

She smiled carefully. "Nothing's changed," she said. "I'm still me—and I'm still interested in hearing about any deal you've cooked up."

"Angelica, you're making more out of this than it's worth."

"In that case, take me with you."

There was a moment's silence, and then Cade shrugged his shoulders.

"Fine," he said. "Come along, if that's what you want."

It was, Angelica was certain, the last thing in the world *Cade* wanted. But she didn't hesitate.

"Thank you," she said with great formality. "I'll be ready in five minutes."

She rose from the bed, still clutching the sheet, and looked at the open boxes lying amid the blankets. She frowned, then scooped up the camisole and panties from the gift box—but she took her own black wool dress from the chair as she walked briskly into the bathroom.

Cade stared after her, his mouth tightening. Then he turned away and poured himself another cup of coffee.

The same Jim Larrabee who'd refused to listen to Angelica's deferred payment plan fell all over himself in his eagerness to agree to Cade's.

What was even worse was the way both men ignored her during the meeting.

"You know Miss Gordon, Jim, " Cade said at its start. Larrabee smiled, shook her hand—and then neither of them looked at her again, not even to ask her opinion before Cade pronounced the deal complete.

That was when Angelica shoved back her chair, got to her feet and stalked from the room.

She was waiting in the car when Cade emerged from the Larrabee offices a few minutes later, staring straight ahead. He opened the door, climbed inside, slammed it shut and threw the car into gear. They went half a dozen blocks in silence, and then he turned to her, glaring.

"Don't you ever embarrass me that way again!"

"*I* embarrassed *you*?" Angelica swung toward him, her face flushed. "You have to be kidding!"

"Look, I don't know what pissed you off, but—"

"I'll tell you what pissed me off! How dare you act as if I'm invisible? You sat there, and that man sat there, and I might as well have been in—in Timbuctoo!"

"Going to that meeting was your idea, lady, not mine!"

"You're damned right. If it had been up to you, I'd never even have known you were planning to meet with Larrabee!"

"Listen, lady—"

"Woman. That's what you call a grown female, Cade. She's not a lady, she's a woman."

"So you keep reminding me. And I guess you're right, because God knows a *lady* would never behave the way you just did."

"You mean, no flower of Western womanhood would ever behave the way I did!"

A horn blared behind them. Cade shot a furious look into the rearview mirror, then stepped on the gas.

"I don't appreciate being made to look like a fool," he said through his teeth.

Angelica sighed dramatically sweetly. "Poor Cade. Was it humiliating to have to explain why I walked out?"

"Not really." His smile was all teeth. "Jim made a joke about PMS and I said, well, for all I knew, he might just be right. You can never tell about women's hormones, can you?"

"That's it! Write this off as something you and the other good ol' boys can laugh about." The car pulled to the curb in front of the hotel. The doorman stepped briskly forward, but Angelica threw the door open before he could reach it. "Having to admit the truth, that you couldn't afford to let me into that discussion because I might just have shown you up, would probably have killed you," she snapped as Cade stepped out of the car and came toward her.

"You? Show me up?" Cade laughed. "Listen, sugar, I don't want to hurt your feelings, but you were in way over your head just sitting there! I can take what you know about this business, stuff it into a thimble and have room left for my finger."

The electric lobby doors swished open as Angelica approached.

"The only thing that was thimble-size in that office was your brain," she said coldly.

"Dammit," Cade snarled. He caught hold of her wrist and swung her toward him. "Don't you think it's time you admitted the truth, *Ms.* Gordon? You don't know the first thing about oil."

"What you mean is, I don't know the first thing about—about going to the bathroom standing up!"

Cade laughed. "Miss Palmer should hear you now, sugar," he said. "I'll bet she'd swoon."

Angelica glared at him. Then she spun on her heel, marched past the reception desk where the clerks were trying their best to pretend nothing out of the ordinary was happening in the posh lobby, and stabbed the call button for the elevator.

"Miss Palmer," she said coldly when Cade caught up to her, "would tell me that I should have known better than to expect you to treat me with respect."

The elevator doors slid open. They stepped inside, and Cade pressed the button for the penthouse floor.

"Angelica," he said. He took a deep breath. "Look, let's not let this get out of hand. I wasn't trying to insult you. It's just that Larrabee and I speak the same language."

"Give me a break, Cade." The doors opened and Angelica stepped into the corridor that led to the suite.

"I hate being patronized. I hate it almost as much as I hate being treated like a—a second-class citizen."

Cade unlocked the door to the sitting room. They stepped inside and he slammed the door after them.

"Will you listen to me, dammit?" He clasped her shoulders and turned her to face him. "In the first place, you don't know a thing about the oil business. That's not an insult, it's fact."

"I'm learning. Besides, I do know about finances, and debt structures, and if you'd only given me a minute or two of your precious time, I could have told you about the plan I'd worked out and offered Mr. Jim Aren't-We-All-Good-Old-Boys Larrabee just a little while ago!"

"It couldn't have been much of a plan, if he turned it down."

"It was a terrific plan, but the person who made it was a woman!"

"Dammit, all you know is what you've read in text-books, and that's not what's happening in the real world!"

Angelica's fists clenched. "It's men like you and Jim Larrabee," she said, her voice trembling, "who won't give me the chance to find out!"

"Angelica . . ."

Cade blew out his breath. Dammit, why were they fighting? She'd made him angry as hell, but that was all draining away, especially now that he saw the telltale glint of tears in her eyes.

OK. Maybe he'd hurt her feelings. But he hadn't meant to; he'd just gone into the meeting the way he always did, ready for the one-on-one kind of thing he was best at, and within seconds he'd been sure that Larrabee was responding positively to it.

Only a fool would have done something to endanger that.

Besides, if he'd thought about Angelica sitting there at all, it had been a quick flash, an awareness that he was putting on one hell of a show and that he had to be dazzling her with how quickly he'd turned Larrabee around.

Instead, he thought, with a twinge of guilt, instead, he'd managed to put those tears in the eyes of—of...

Cade's heart kicked against his ribs. He'd put tears in the eyes of the only woman he'd ever loved.

Angelica had turned away from him. Her head was bowed; she looked fragile and vulnerable, and his throat constricted.

"Angel," he said softly. He reached out and touched her shoulder gently. "Angel, I'm sorry. You're right."

She turned and looked at him. "Do you mean it?" she said, and wiped the back of her hand across her eyes.

"Yes, of course." He smiled and drew her toward him. "I don't ever want us to quarrel again."

She smiled, too, shakily. He could feel the tension in her body giving way.

"Me neither," she whispered. "It's just—the thing is, you made me feel so useless..."

Cade nodded. "I know."

"There I sat, the head of the Gordon Oil Company, and—"

"Well, sure." He smiled. "That was part of the problem. We should have straightened all that out before we went into that meeting, but I figured you weren't quite ready to admit that you weren't really the head of Gordon Oil, so—"

Angelica pulled back and stared at him. "What do you mean? I never said—"

"Angel. We both know there never was a verbal agreement."

She swallowed dryly. "Oh?"

"But I can understand that what happens to the company is important to you. Hell, it belonged to your father." Cade threaded his fingers into her hair and tilted her face to his. "Tell you what. I'll direct whoever I put in charge to send me special periodic reports on the company's progress, and—"

"You mean—you mean, you're taking the company away from me?"

"Angel, you know that's what I came here to do."

"But—but you just said—you said you were sorry, that I was right, that it was men like you who were keeping me from getting a feel for the business—"

Cade frowned. "I never said anything like that."

"You did, Cade! You said you'd help me learn—"

"Hell, you're twisting everything." His frown deepened. "I said I shouldn't have let you go into that meeting thinking you were still in charge of Gordon Oil, that I should have told you—"

"You mean—you mean, you'd already reached a decision this morning?"

"Angel, you aren't listening. I've just told you, I knew all along you had to be lying about that verbal agreement." He smiled. "Oh, I was willing to figure there might be a chance in a million that it was real, but—"

"But instead of telling me that," Angelica said, "you decided to play games." Her voice shook. "You—you held out hope when there wasn't any, you—you seduced me..."

"Will you stop this?" Cade's eyes darkened with anger; he grabbed her by the arms and shook her. "Forget Gordon Oil, dammit! I love you, Angelica. Do you hear me? I love you, and you don't need Gordon Oil anymore. I'll take care of you for the rest of your life."

For a fraction of a second, the admission that he loved her seemed to shimmer in the air between them. But then it was swept aside, made meaningless by reality.

"You mean—you mean, you'll do what you did today, Cade, you'll—you'll treat me like—like some poor little soul who's incapable of thinking for herself."

"No!" His fingers bit into her flesh. "I'll treat you like the woman you really are. I'll cherish you and protect you—"

"And think for me, and speak for me..." The breath sobbed from Angelica's throat. She gave an anguished cry as she twisted free of his grasp. "I'd sooner die than live my life like that!"

Cade's mouth thinned. "Let me be sure we understand each other," he said. "If I gave you the choice between running Gordon Oil and marrying me—"

"This hasn't anything to do with Gordon Oil! Don't you see? I need to be my own person, Cade, I need to have the right to—to make my own decisions."

"Then make one," he said, his eyes fixed to hers. "Marry me and give up all this crap—or I'll walk out of your life forever and give you your precious company as a parting gift."

Angelica stared at him, her eyes wide with anguish. "Cade," she whispered, "I love you. You can't mean—"

"I do mean," he said grimly, even while a little voice deep within him whispered that this scene had been played before, that he was like a man caught in a time warp, doomed to repeat history with only a change in the cast of characters. "I mean every word. Now, make a decision, and make it fast."

She spun away from him, hoping that he was only testing her, waiting for some word from him to soften the cruel choice he'd given her.

But the moments slipped away, leaving only silence behind.

At last she turned and looked at him. Tears trembled on her lashes.

"Cade," she said, her voice anguished, "Cade, please..."

His face turned to stone. "I'll have the papers drawn up," he said. "Goodbye, Angelica."

He walked to the bedroom, shut the door after him, and just that quickly, it was over.

CHAPTER TEN

SOMEWHERE in the skies halfway to London, Cade calmed down enough to realize that the moment of high drama he'd created in that Dallas hotel suite had really been an exercise in low comedy.

He couldn't give Angelica Gordon that damned oil company.

It wasn't his to give.

But he'd sooner have burned in the fires of hell than pull back from that stupid pledge. It was a matter of pride, and pride was about all he had left right now.

What a fool he'd made of himself. And what an ass he'd been to have ever imagined himself in love with Angelica.

Him? In love with a woman like that? Cade almost laughed out loud. That he'd thought such a thing only proved he'd spent too many of the past months in the world's backwaters. The women of Dumai were gorgeous—but evidently he'd missed the homegrown variety more than he'd realized.

Angelica had been the first long-legged American female he'd seen in months. And, he had to admit, her initial coldness had been a challenge.

Yes sir, he thought as he sipped his third bourbon and water, it had definitely been a surefire recipe for disaster.

Thank God he was safely out of it!

Cade smiled to himself. London was going to be terrific. He loved the place, all that up-to-date energy mixed with the still-majestic reminders of a glowing past. And the women—ah, the women were special, with their

English-rose complexions and their joy in their femininity.

It would take him all of an hour to forget the Dallas mess, once he was on English soil—if he could just figure a way to hand that damned directorship to Angelica Gordon. Then he'd never have to think about her again.

He took another sip of his drink. He could always come clean with his brothers, tell them what had happened....

No. Grant and Zach would cackle with laughter at his idiocy. Besides, why should they take the fall for him? Landon Enterprises was worth less on the market with Gordon Oil dragging it down. Why should his brothers lose money because he—

Of course! Cade began to grin. The solution was painfully simple.

He would buy Gordon's from Landon Enterprises; the directorship would be his to give away then—and his accountant might even love him for having come up with a tax loss.

The flight attendant came hurrying as soon as he pressed the call button.

"Yes, Mr. Landon," she said, smiling prettily. "May I get you something? Another drink, perhaps?"

Her smile suggested that she might happily do more, if he only asked.

Cade looked at her. She was very pretty, he thought, very pretty indeed—if you liked hazel eyes and straight, blond hair. But he didn't. He preferred eyes the color of emeralds, hair that was touched with fire....

Dammit, he thought, and he scowled so darkly that the flight attendant drew back.

"I want a telephone," he said brusquely, "and fast."

His first call was to Grant in New York. His older brother heard him out, then laughed.

"Are you nuts? You can't buy Gordon Oil. We already own it."

"You're not listening," Cade said impatiently. "I want to buy it from Landon Enterprises. Is that possible?"

"Anything's possible. But why? The company's a dog."

"I have my reasons," Cade said—and waited for the practical Grant to demand, and be denied, a list of those reasons.

But Grant only muttered something about insanity evidently running in the family, and said that if that was what Cade wanted, he'd start working on it.

Cade frowned. "That's it? You're not going to give me a hard time?"

Grant gave a choked laugh. "I'm not up to giving anybody a hard time lately," he said. "Call Zach. Ask him what he needs to work up an idea of what we should charge you for Gordon Oil. I'll get back to you."

Cade's call to Hollywood took Zach out of a meeting.

"I've got something important going on here," he growled. "So make it fast."

Cade explained what he wanted.

"Are you crazy?" Zach said. "Why in hell would you buy that company?"

"That's my business. You just tell me what you need to work up a purchase price."

Zach gave a harsh laugh. "I bet it's got something to do with that woman who's running it."

Cade frowned. "Don't be ridiculous. Why would you say that?"

His brother's sigh was deep enough to cross the Atlantic on its own.

"No reason," he said hollowly, "no reason at all. OK, get in touch with Denver. Have them phone me and I'll tell them what I need."

"Can you do this quickly?"

"Sure, assuming Denver holds up its end. But without Bayliss—"

Cade's mouth thinned. "Yeah," he said, and hung up. He sat motionless for a moment, then rang for the flight attendant again.

"Did you need something else, sir?" she said with a hopeful smile.

Cade didn't smile at all. "Yes," he said grimly. "I need to know how fast I can get from London to Denver."

He was exhausted by the time he reached Denver, working on a fine edge of airline coffee, lack of sleep and a simmering anger that had overtaken him on the endless flight home.

He climbed into a taxi, told the driver where to take him and lay his head back.

He was supposed to be in London. Instead, he was back in the States.

He was supposed to be finalizing plans for a North Sea drilling expedition. Instead, he was arranging to buy a dying oil firm—and if his brothers or anybody else ever found out the reason, he'd never live it down.

Angelica, he thought, Angelica was to blame for all of this.

How could one woman have messed up his life so thoroughly in so short a time?

Cade's jaw tightened. The sooner he closed the books on this brief and not-so-shining episode in his life, the better.

Kyra was surprised to see him, and pleased—but Cade sensed a kind of removal, just as he had with Grant and Zach.

"Squirt?" he said as he was heading to his bedroom. "Are you OK?"

"Sure. I'm fine."

"Have you been eating right?" He frowned. "You always did skip meals. Maybe you're not getting enough vitamins or—"

"Cade," Kyra said gently, "why don't you do us both a favor and stop thinking for me?"

Cade's mouth twisted. "What is this? The new female battle cry?"

Kyra gave him a long look and then she sighed. "Get some sleep," she said. "We'll talk when you're back among the living."

Cade didn't argue. His brain was barely functioning; he made it up the steps and into his room, and collapsed on the bed.

He awoke confused after a long, rambling dream that had involved a woman with a mane of copper curls. He'd chased her for hours across what had looked like the Texas flats, only to catch her, turn her in his arms—and discover that she wasn't anyone he knew.

He sat up, flexed his shoulders and rubbed his hands across his face. He needed a shower and a shave and then—assuming he could find the energy—he'd go to the Landon offices, phone Zach and begin pulling together the materials he needed.

When he came downstairs, Kyra was waiting for him, along with a platter of bacon and eggs, a stack of toast and a pot of coffee.

"What?" he said, smiling. "No groaning sideboard? No obscene breakfast buffet?"

Kyra smiled, too. "I'm going to be making some changes," she said. "Go on, eat. You're looking at that food like a starving man."

Cade laughed. "I must have had a meal sometime in the past twenty-four hours, but if I did, I sure as hell don't remember it."

When he was done, he sat back and sighed with pleasure. "That was terrific, Squirt. One more cup of coffee, and then I'm off."

"To where?"

"To the office."

"For what?"

"I have to pull some papers from the files."

"Why?"

Cade's brows lifted. "Squirt," he said patiently, "it's business. You wouldn't understand."

Kyra's lips tightened. "Try me."

"Sis, look, I know you mean well, but—"

"But what? Is it too complicated for my pretty head?"

Cade threw down his napkin. "What the hell is going on here? I tell you right now, I've had a bellyful of this crap!"

"Well, so have I." His sister glared at him. "Women don't like to be treated like—like dolls."

"And men don't like to be despised for trying to show they care. If a man didn't love a woman, he wouldn't..."

Cade clamped his lips together. Then he shoved back his chair and got to his feet. "If Zach or Grant calls, tell them they can reach me at the office."

Kyra nodded. "Yes, sir," she said sweetly.

Cade stormed out the door.

It took almost a week for Cade to get all the information to Zach and for Zach to comb through it. But, at last, he telephoned.

"OK," he said, "we're almost there."

"What do you mean, almost? I sent you everything in the files."

"Yeah. Some interesting stuff, too. That woman who's been running Gordon's? She's made some clever suggestions about restructuring the company's debts. I'm impressed."

I do know about finances and debt structures, and if you'd only given me a minute or two of your precious time...

"Never mind being impressed," Cade said sharply. "Just give me a buyout price."

"I will, but I'll need some updated figures first."

"Dammit, Zach, just come up with a number! Any number!"

"I don't do business that way, Cade, and neither does any man in his right mind. Look, what's the big deal? Call Dallas, talk to a secretary or a clerk—"

"I don't have to talk to the Gordon woman?"

"No, of course not. Half a dozen quick questions, and that's it."

A muscle knotted in Cade's jaw. "That's it?"

"You got it, brother. Twenty-four hours later, you'll own Gordon Oil."

Twenty-four hours later, Cade thought as he hung up the phone, he could forget about Angelica Gordon forever.

He dreamed again that night, some hellish nightmare that had him racing down a dark corridor, banging open doors but never finding the one thing his hammering heart told him he must find...

...the one woman he must find...

"Angelica?" he said, as he shot bolt upright in bed.

After a moment, he shoved back the covers and got to his feet. It had snowed outside, the first snow of the season, and the land lay white and still in the moonlight. He stood at the window, looking at the night sky, wondering if there were any chance Angelica might be looking at the same moon and feeling what he felt, this awful emptiness where his heart should have been.

"Damn," he whispered, and pounded his fist into his hand.

He didn't love her. He had never loved her—and she sure as hell had never loved him. The only thing she loved was some hardheaded, selfish dream.

He pulled on a pair of jeans and an old sweatshirt. Barefoot, he made his way through the sleeping house to the kitchen. He hadn't wanted a cup of hot chocolate in years, but tonight...

Moonlight illuminated the figure of his sister. Dressed in a long flannel nightgown, Kyra sat curled on the cushioned sill of the big bay window that overlooked the mountains.

"What are you doing up?" Cade said. "It's late. And it's cold down here. You should be wearing a robe, and..." He frowned and cleared his throat. "Kyra? Do I—ah, do I do that a lot? Am I, uh, do I tend to be overly protective?"

She smiled gently. "You mean, are you like Father?"

"What? No! Of course not. I'm nothing like the old man. Hell, I'd never—"

"Oh, you're not anywhere near as dominating, and you're certainly not selfish." She put her hand on his. "But you do like to control."

Cade pulled his hand away. "That's ridiculous."

"Maybe you think control and protection are the same, that you have to control somebody in order to take care of them and love them."

"Great God almighty!" Cade slammed his hands onto his hips. "Don't tell me I've run into another believer in the joys of psychology!"

"Or maybe, down deep, you think you have to control someone to keep them from abandoning you."

"What?"

"I wonder if it could have something to do with what happened the night of your twenty-first birthday?"

"What in hell are you talking about?"

"Oh, Cade." Kyra's voice was soft. "You know you've never forgotten. That girl who left you—Casey? Lacey?"

"Stacey," Cade snapped, "and what would you know about it? You were just a baby."

"I was fifteen," Kyra said with a little smile. "Hardly a baby. I knew how hurt you were."

Cade flushed. "I wasn't hurt, I was ticked off. Hell, I was only a kid."

"Come on, admit it. Losing her that way must have left a hole in your heart. Someday you'll meet a woman..." His sister looked at him, her eyes wise beyond her years. "Or have you met her already?" she asked gently. "Is that what's put the shadows in your eyes?"

Cade glared at her. "Thank you, Dr. Freud," he snarled. "Your brilliant analysis has been more than helpful."

He pivoted on his heel and marched from the room. Kyra watched him go, and then she sighed.

"You did ask," she whispered, and turned her face to the window.

Zach had said Cade only needed to phone the Gordon office for the final information.

But in the morning, Cade boarded the earliest flight he could get for Dallas.

In the long run, it would be quicker, he told himself; he could get the stuff he needed straight from Emily without any possibility of a slipup, and if he called ahead, he could do it at a time when Angelica would be out of the office.

But somehow, he forgot to make the call before he left Denver. He forgot to make it when he reached the airport in Dallas, and it even slipped his mind to call from the cellular phone in his rental car.

Well, it didn't matter. Seeing Angelica again wouldn't bother him at all, he told himself as he pushed open the door to the Gordon office, and if Angelica didn't like it, that was just too damned—

"Yes? May I help you, sir?"

Cade stared at the woman seated behind the reception desk.

"You're not Emily," he said.

She smiled politely. "Emily's not here anymore."

"She isn't?"

"No, sir. She took a position at another firm. May I help you?"

Cade looked at the closed door to Angelica's office. "Yes," he said, "yes, you may. My name is Cade Landon, and—"

"From Landon Enterprises?" The woman rose to her feet. "What a coincidence, sir. I was just about to post this letter to your Denver office, and—"

"Is—is Ms. Gordon in?" he said. He took a step toward Angelica's door and then he stopped. "Not that I wish to see her," he said, frowning, "but—"

"No, sir. She's not."

Cade cleared his throat. "Yes, well, that's all right. I'm sure you can help me with—"

"I'm afraid Ms. Gordon doesn't work here anymore."

Cade swung toward the woman. "What?"

"It's all in this letter, Mr. Landon. Ms. Gordon resigned. She told me to post this first thing this morning, and—"

"That's impossible," Cade said sharply. "She couldn't have resigned."

"Well, she did. She hired a replacement, of course, if you wish to meet him..."

"Let me see that letter," Cade said, and grabbed it from her.

He read it through, but it said nothing; it might as well have been a form resignation copied straight from a business manual.

"When did she leave?" he snapped, and tossed the letter on the desk.

"Well, on Friday, sir. I mean, that was when she left the office. But I don't think she left Dallas until Saturday, or perhaps—"

The woman gasped as Cade caught her by the arms. "She left Dallas?"

"Yes, sir."

"Where did she go? Dammit, woman..."

"My name is Carlisle, sir. Alice Carlisle."

"Ms. Carlisle," Cade said. "Alice." He took a deep breath, lifted his hands from her and stepped back. "This is very important, Alice. I must find Ms. Gordon. I have to find her, and tell her—and tell her..." He smiled, or hoped he did. God only knew if he were smiling or grimacing in pain. "Do you know where she's gone?"

"Why, she went home, of course. Some town in Connecticut, Mr. Landon. I have it right here...."

Cade snatched the slip of paper from Alice Carlisle's hand. His eyes skimmed the address, and then he turned and hurried from the office.

CHAPTER ELEVEN

THE LITTLE town of Eastgate, Connecticut, was picture-postcard beautiful, a traditional bit of New England that might have been created by an artist—or an overly zealous Chamber of Commerce.

Clapboard saltboxes with dark slate roofs stood sentinel around the village square. In summer, the square was a verdant green; now, in late autumn, the maples and oaks that lined it had shed their leaves, covering the grass with a carpet of crimson and gold. A church flanked the square, its spare lines an acknowledgment of its Puritan ancestry, its white steeple reaching toward the sky, the golden spire catching the last, sharp light of the late afternoon sun.

A block north of the square, a column of stately elms lined the cobbled driveway that led to the handsome Gothic structure that was Miss Palmer's Academy. The original stone building had been extended over the years so that now it was a large and imposing edifice. Beyond its west wing, a breeze delicately ruffled the waters of Eastgate Pond, where the young ladies of the academy swam in the languid heat of summer and ice skated in the brisk chill of the New England winter.

Angelica sighed as she gazed down on the scene from the gentle rise on which she stood.

It was a perfect picture, she thought, just as she'd thought so many times before—and she waited for the rush of pleasure that should have accompanied the knowledge that she was back where she belonged.

But the feeling wouldn't come.

She had arrived yesterday, spent the night at the Eastgate Inn and met with the academy's headmistress this afternoon. Miss James had been gracious. The school would be delighted to have Angelica back, she'd said; her old position would be waiting for her at the start of the next semester.

Her friends on the academy staff had greeted her warmly. No one had questioned her return; everyone simply hugged her and said how wonderful it was to have her back.

"You're home again," Jack Brenner had said, whirling her around in a circle.

Then, why was there this awful heaviness in her heart?

This place, this familiar part of the States, *was* home. And Jack and Miss James and the others were not just friends, they were her kind of people. They spoke the same language, had the same expectations...

And yet, every time Angelica smiled, she felt as if she were forcing her face to assume an alien mask. Every time she said yes, she was very happy to be back, she felt as if she were speaking a lie.

And it was all Cade's fault, damn him! It was all because he'd ended up being the contemptible, insensitive, chauvinistic bastard she'd pegged him for from the beginning.

At least she wasn't still in love with him, she thought, lifting her chin—if, indeed, she ever had been. The more she thought about it, the more convinced she was that she, of all people, had ended up believing the hoary old wive's tale that said a woman always fell in love with the man to whom she gave her virginity.

Yes, she thought, that had to be it. She'd fed herself romantic propaganda rather than accept the truth, which was that what had happened between her and Cade was nothing but meaningless sex...

"Angelica?"

Angelica frowned. Jack, she thought, with a twinge of guilt. He'd gone walking with her, and somehow she'd forgotten all about him.

She moistened her lips, fixed them in a smile and turned to him.

"Jack, I'm terribly sorry." She put her hand on his arm. "I must have been daydreaming."

"There's no need to apologize." Jack took her hand in his. "I understand how you must feel, Angelica. It must be wonderful, being back home again."

Angelica nodded. "It is," she said quickly. "It's—it's wonderful."

Jack laced his fingers through hers and they began walking slowly along the crest of the hill.

"I like what you've done with your hair," he said, smiling at her.

She laughed and put her hand to the long, loose curls the breeze was gently tossing against her shoulders.

"I guess I finally figured out that there's no point trying to disguise myself, Jack. I am who I am, and that's that."

He grinned. "Sounds good to me." His hand tightened on hers. "I just can't tell you how glad I am to see you again."

"And I'm glad to see you, too." Angelica sighed. "It's just that—I don't know, it seems impossible that I'm back here in Eastgate."

"Yes. It seems that way to me, too. I'd really begun to think we'd lost you forever."

Angelica's smile tilted. "Nothing is forever, Jack," she said. "That's one thing I've learned these past months."

"I'll bet your exile in Siberia must have seemed like forever," Jack said, and grinned.

Angelica grinned back at him. "That's another thing I learned. Believe it or not, Texas is part of the United States."

"Maybe—and then again, maybe not." Jack made a sweeping gesture that took in the town nestled below them. "But it can't compare to this."

"Well, it's entirely different than this. New England is beautiful. But Texas—Texas is beautiful, too."

"I suppose." They strolled along in companionable silence, and then Jack glanced at her. "So," he said quietly, "I take it that the Dallas thing didn't work out?"

Angelica shook her head. "No. No, it didn't."

"I'm sorry. I'm sure it wasn't anything you did—"

"I made a lot of mistakes, Jack. I realize that now."

Jack put his hands lightly on Angelica's shoulders and turned her toward him.

"But it's over with, right? You sold your dad's company?"

"Oh, it wasn't mine to sell. It turned out he'd sold it himself, before he died. I just—I ran it for a while, and then—and then the conglomerate that had bought it from my father sent somebody down to check things out, and—and..."

"And what?" Jack frowned. "Don't tell me he fired you?"

"No. Well, he was going to, but...but he ended up offering to let me stay on."

"For how long?"

Angelica took a deep breath. "For—for as long as I wanted."

Jack gave an uncertain laugh. "I'm lost here, Angelica. This corporate pencil pusher came down to give you the once-over, and—"

"He wasn't a pencil pusher," she said quickly.

"Whatever. He looked things over, liked what you were doing—so why'd you quit?"

"He didn't. Like what I was doing, I mean. He—he said I didn't know anything about the oil business."

Jack grimaced. "Sounds like a typical chauvinist to me."

"No!" Angelica shook her head. "No, he was right. I didn't know anything about the business. That's why I was screwing up."

Jack gave a puzzled laugh. "So he offered to keep you on as director for as long as you wanted?" He grinned and chucked her under the chin. "I must be missing something here."

Angelica stared at him. Yes, she thought, oh, yes, he was definitely missing something. He was missing the part that mattered, where Cade had demanded she make a cold-blooded choice between his selfish idea of love and her need to feel whole.

But she would never feel whole again. Never, because without Cade—without his love...

A choked sound burst from her throat. Jack stared at her.

"Angelica?" he said.

He reached toward her but she shook her head fiercely and swung away from him. Tears rose in her eyes as she stared blindly out over the village.

She loved Cade. Lord, how she loved him! And she always would, no matter how many long, empty years went by.

How could Cade have been such a fool? How could he have imagined she'd choose the directorship of Gordon Oil over a life at his side?

Would he ever suspect that leaving Gordon Oil had been the easiest thing she'd ever done in her life?

It was living without Cade that was going to be hard. Impossible, maybe, if the last week was any indication. She'd spent it in such misery, lying awake at night and aching for the feel of his strong, comforting arms, waking in the morning and not opening her eyes so she could pretend that loving him and losing him had all been a bad dream . . .

"Angelica?" Jack's hands clasped her shoulders and he turned her toward him. "What's wrong? Please, tell me."

She tried to smile her reassurance, but it didn't work. The tears only came faster. Jack put his arms around her. She let him draw her close and bring her head against his chest.

Please, she thought, please let me feel safe, and secure, and happy.

But she felt none of those things. Jack was a good man, a kind man, and though she'd never admitted it to herself before, she knew that he was close to falling in love with her.

They were a perfect match. They held the same convictions. He respected her as an equal; he would never dream of doing anything without seeking her opinion first—and she would need that from a man before she could make a life with him, she knew that.

The trouble was that she'd have to have other things, too. He'd have to make her blood sing just by touching her, his kisses would have to turn her to flame, and just the sight of him or the sound of his voice would have to fill her with a joy so fierce it was almost painful.

"Angelica?"

She went rigid in Jack's arms. Was she so unhappy, so lost without Cade, that she'd taken to imagining the sound of his voice?

"Angelica."

Time seemed to stop. She pulled a deep, shuddering breath into her lungs and put her hands against Jack's chest. Slowly, his embrace loosened and she turned in his arms.

A tremor went through her.

"Cade," she whispered.

He looked much as he had that day at the Odessa wells, standing tall and handsome in a leather jacket, jeans and boots...

Her heart felt as if it might burst.

"Cade? What—what are you doing here?"

He moved slowly toward her, his eyes never leaving her face.

"I came to see you," he said softly. "And to tell you—to tell you..." He looked away from her then, at Jack.

Angelica looked at Jack, too. He was staring at Cade as if he'd seen an apparition, and just for an instant Angelica smiled as she thought how each must be sizing up the other and trying to make sense out of what he saw.

"Jack," she said, "this is—this is Cade Landon. He—he..." He's the man I love, the man I'll always love, she almost said, but she had at least some pride left. "He—he's the man I was telling you about, the one who—who offered to let me stay on at my father's oil company."

"But you didn't," Cade said, his eyes meeting hers again.

Angelica sighed. "No."

Cade took another step forward. "Why?" he said softly. "It was what you wanted, Angel, what you wanted more than anything else in the world."

"Did I ever say that?"

Cade's eyes narrowed. "You didn't have to. You made it clear enough."

Her chin trembled. "Cade Landon," she said, "you are the biggest damned fool..."

Tears rose in her eyes again and she spun away from him.

"Angelica?" Jack cleared his throat. "Angelica, what's going on here?"

She rubbed her hand across her eyes, hating herself for breaking down, hating Cade for whatever pound of flesh he'd come to collect—and feeling nothing but compassion for Jack, who looked like a man who'd found himself trapped inside a maze without a clue as to how he'd got there.

"I'm sorry," she said. "Jack, I'm so sorry, but—but..."

Jack looked from Angelica to Cade. "I understand," he said, and he smiled a little sadly. "At least stop by and say goodbye before you leave, Angelica. Will you do that?"

Angelica looked at him as if he were crazy. "I'm not going anywhere."

Jack nodded. "Right," he said. He put his hand against her cheek in a last, gentle caress. Then he nodded at Cade, brushed past him and strode down the hill.

Cade waited until the other man was barely a pinpoint in the distance. Then he frowned and turned to Angelica.

"An old flame?"

"A good friend."

"For somebody who's just a friend, he was holding you pretty damn close."

Angelica's chin lifted. "He's a very good friend. Besides, it's none of your business."

"All right, then, let's try something that *is* my business. Why did you give up your job at Gordon Oil?"

She stared at him, and then she turned away, tucked her hands into the pockets of her jacket and started walking. He fell in beside her.

"An employee only has to give notice, not a reason for resigning a position."

Cade's lips twitched. "What textbook is that from?"

"I don't owe you any explanations, Cade. I'm not asking for severance pay or even a reference."

"And a good thing," he growled, "considering that you don't know a damned thing about running an oil company."

Angelica spun toward him, her eyes flashing. "Are we back to that? Anyway, I never said I did!"

Cade smiled. "No. You didn't." He looked at her. "But you do know something about finance and debt structure."

"You're damned right I do! I..." She frowned. "Who says so?"

Cade's lips twitched again. "You did, if I'm remembering right. Well, and my brother says so, too."

"Your brother!" Angelica tossed her head. "Another Landon genius, no doubt."

"I wouldn't call Zach a genius—not to his face, anyway." Cade grinned. "But he's got a pretty fair reputation as a guy who knows how to take a little bit of money and coax it into a lot."

"And he said that I..." Angelica smiled sweetly. "Are you sure he knows I'm a woman? That might change his attitude considerably."

Cade took a deep breath. "I'm the one who needs the change of attitude," he said, "the one who needs to remember that you can be my woman and still be your own person."

Angelica stared at him. "What?"

He smiled. "I think you might find that you and my sister, Kyra, have a great deal in common."

"I don't—I don't understand. What does your sister have to do with me?"

"Nothing." He moved closer to her, and the way he looked into her eyes made it almost impossible for her to breathe. "Nothing—and everything. She's a very wise young woman, that sister of mine. It turns out she knows things about me that I..." Cade took a deep breath. "Angel," he said softly. He reached out, framed Angelica's face in his hands. "Angel, I love you. I love you with all my heart."

Angelica's lips trembled. What was the sense in denying the truth?

"Oh, Cade," she whispered, "I love you, too. I always will—but it won't work."

"It will," he said, with that wonderful strength and determination she knew so well. "I've learned a lot in the past week, Angel. For instance, I know now that the only way to keep you is to let you have your freedom."

Hope blossomed in Angelica's heart. "Not too much freedom," she said, her eyes on his. "I've learned some things too, Cade, that—that love can make you stronger, not weaker, that I've never been happier than when you're holding me in your arms."

Cade smiled and gathered her to him. "I'll make you an offer, Angel."

"What offer?" she whispered.

He brushed his mouth gently over hers. "I'm flying to London in a couple of days. Come with me."

"Come with—"

"Yes. Zach says you've got a head for figures. Well, frankly, I'm better at what happens in the field than I am with what happens on a balance sheet. I'll teach you about the oil business and you can teach me finance— and after we put the London deal to bed, we'll come home and make a success of Gordon Oil."

Angelica stared at him. "Are you serious?"

"Yes." He frowned. "Although there are two conditions."

Her smile dimmed. "What conditions?"

Cade put his hand under her chin and tilted her face to his.

"The first is that you have to tell me you love me."

She smiled and linked her arms around his neck. "Of course I love you, you arrogant, opinionated, impossible man. If you weren't so pigheaded, you'd have figured that out long ago."

"Like the first time we made love, you mean." Cade drew her close. "You'd never had a lover before me, had you, sweetheart?"

A soft blush spread over Angelica's cheeks. "You were my first lover, Cade," she said softly.

"And your last," he said in whisper so fierce it thrilled her. He kissed her and then looked into her eyes. "So, what do you think? Would you like to come with me to London, then come back to the States and help me run Gordon Oil?"

"You said there were *two* conditions."

"Absolutely." Cade framed her face in his hands. "You have to love me—and you have to marry me, Angel. Otherwise, the deal's off."

Angelica leaned back in Cade's arms. His expression was unyielding; it gave nothing away. But when she looked into his eyes, she could see the sweetly teasing laughter there.

"I don't know," she said. "That's an awful lot to ask of a woman."

He kissed her again, a long, deep kiss that stole her breath away.

"I love you, sweetheart," he said. "And I always will."

Angelica smiled. "You'd better," she whispered, and then she kissed him with all the love that had been so long pent-up inside her heart.

* * * * *

If you enjoyed this book, watch out next month for GUARDIAN GROOM by Sandra Marton, in which we meet Cade's brother Grant—and his irresistible ward, Christa...

UNLOCK THE DOOR TO GREAT ROMANCE AT BRIDE'S BAY RESORT

Join Harlequin's new across-the-lines series, set in an exclusive hotel on an island off the coast of South Carolina.

Seven of your favorite authors will bring you exciting stories about fascinating heroes and heroines discovering love at Bride's Bay Resort.

Look for these fabulous stories coming to a store near you beginning in January 1996.

Harlequin American Romance #613 in January
Matchmaking Baby by Cathy Gillen Thacker

Harlequin Presents #1794 in February
Indiscretions by Robyn Donald

Harlequin Intrigue #362 in March
Love and Lies by Dawn Stewardson

Harlequin Romance #3404 in April
Make Believe Engagement by Day Leclaire

Harlequin Temptation #588 in May
Stranger in the Night by Roseanne Williams

Harlequin Superromance #695 in June
Married to a Stranger by Connie Bennett

Harlequin Historicals #324 in July
Dulcie's Gift by Ruth Langan

Visit Bride's Bay Resort each month wherever
Harlequin books are sold.

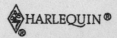

MILLION DOLLAR SWEEPSTAKES

SWP-M96

HARLEQUIN ❖ PRESENTS®

—where satisfaction is guaranteed!

Coming next month, two classic stories
by your favorite authors:

FORGOTTEN HUSBAND
by Helen Bianchin
Harlequin Presents #1809

They said he was her husband...

But Elise didn't feel married to Alejandro Santanas, or
the mother of his unborn child. The accident had destroyed
her memory of the past few months. Had she really been in
love with this handsome stranger—and would he expect
that passion again?

ONE NIGHT OF LOVE
by Sally Wentworth
Harlequin Presents #1810

Once bitten, twice shy!

Oliver Balfour was the most attractive man Dyan had ever
met. But she wasn't going to mix business with pleasure.
From experience Dyan knew that a man like Oliver
would stalk a woman like her by lying his way into her
affections...and then go quickly for the kill in her bed!

Harlequin Presents—the best has just gotten better!
Available in May wherever Harlequin books are sold.

Fall in love all over again with

This Time... Marriage

In this collection of original short stories, three brides get a unique chance for a return engagement!

- Being kidnapped from your bridal shower by a one-time love can really put a crimp in your wedding plans! *The Borrowed Bride*— by **Susan Wiggs**, *Romantic Times* Career Achievement Award-winning author.

- After fifteen years a couple reunites for the sake of their child—this time will it end in marriage? *The Forgotten Bride*—by **Janice Kaiser**.

- It's tough to make a good divorce stick—especially when you're thrown together with your ex in a magazine wedding shoot! *The Bygone Bride*— by **Muriel Jensen**.

Don't miss THIS TIME...MARRIAGE, available in April wherever Harlequin books are sold.

You're About to Become a
Privileged Woman

Reap the rewards of fabulous free gifts and benefits with proofs-of-purchase from Harlequin and Silhouette books

Pages & Privileges™

It's our way of thanking you for buying our books at your favorite retail stores.

Pages & Privileges ™

✂

PROOF OF PURCHASE

HP-PP120

Offer expires October 31, 1996

**Harlequin and Silhouette—
the most privileged readers in the world!**

For more information about Harlequin and Silhouette's PAGES & PRIVILEGES program call the Pages & Privileges Benefits Desk: 1-503-794-2499

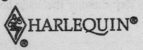

◆ HARLEQUIN®

HP-PP120